PRINCE JAN
ST. BERNARD

" 'The duty of a St. Bernard is to save lives and be worthy of his
ancestors.' "

PRINCE JAN

ST. BERNARD

*How a Dog from the Land of Snow Made
Good in the Land of No Snow*

BY

FORRESTINE C. HOOKER

The Sun Dial Press, Inc.

GARDEN CITY, NEW YORK

J

H76p

TO

AN AMERICAN PATRIOT

My father, Brigadier-General Charles L. Cooper, U. S. A., whose life for fifty-seven years, from May 27, 1862 to September 30, 1919, when he answered the Last Roll Call, was devoted to the service of his Country and his Flag.

F. C. H.

CONTENTS

CONTENTS

LIST OF ILLUSTRATIONS

PRINCE JAN
ST. BERNARD

PRINCE JAN
St. Bernard

Chapter I

THE HOSPICE DOGS

PRINCE JAN was a fuzzy, woolly puppy with clumsy paws and fat, round body covered with tawny hair. His brown eyes looked with loving good-will at everything and everybody.

Jan and his brother, Rollo, had great fun playing together, his long fur making it easy for Rollo to haul him around, while Jan's teeth slipped from his brother's short hair. Though they tumbled about and growled fiercely at each other, their eyes were dancing with laughter.

When tired of playing, they would coax their mother to tell them stories about the Hospice dogs. Then they would lie very quietly listening with pricked-up ears and earnest eyes. Some-

1

times Bruno, the oldest dog in the kennels, would join in the talk, and all the young dogs would gather around to hear the history of their family. Prince Jan and Rollo, cuddled beside their mother, would look at each other with pride, remembering that they, too, were St. Bernards.

"I have heard the monks tell visitors that our ancestors have lived in the Hospice for a thousand years," said Bruno in one of his talks. "When you puppies are old enough, you will be trained for work. The duty of a St. Bernard dog is to save lives and be worthy of his ancestors."

Jan and Rollo looked at him and thumped their tails to show that they understood.

"A good St. Bernard dog must have a sensitive nose, sturdy legs, and keen brains," Bruno's voice was very sober. "He knows what he must do when he finds a human being lost in the storm or frozen in the snow. Then he leads the way to the Hospice, or if the traveller does not follow, the dog brings monks to aid the man. Should one of us ever fail to do his best," he turned his big head slowly and his eyes were serious as he looked at the puppies, "it would mean disgrace for all the rest of the St. Bernard dogs."

"Tell us more stories, Bruno," the youngsters begged.

"Not to-day," Bruno shook his wise head. "Your ancestors have done great things, and you have the right to be proud of them, but the only way to prove yourselves worthy is for you to do your duty as well as they did theirs. Unless you remember your lessons and follow them, you will not be true St. Bernards, and your failures will be stains on the honor of the name we bear. Never forget that as long as you live!"

Bruno understood that the soft little whimpers were promises that each puppy would do his best when the test came to him. Jan and Rollo watched the old dog, limping from rheumatism in his shoulders, move slowly across the enclosed yard that opened from the kennels. Bruno was no longer able to go out on the trails, but spent his days teaching the young dogs. Sometimes he would lie asleep, and when his paws jerked and his tail moved, Jan's mother would say, "Be quiet, children! Bruno is dreaming he is out on the trail."

Then she would speak softly, "When you are older you will be taught to break trails through the snow and carry food and wine, fastened about your necks. You may be tempted, when the wind howls and the snow blinds you, to sneak back or hide in a sheltered place. You must not forget, as long as you live, that there was never a traitor or coward in your father's family or in mine. When you remember this, you will stagger on or crawl, if you cannot stand, and keep your nose close to the ground, sniffing and sniffing."

She turned her head toward the white peaks that loomed high above the stone walls around the enclosure. "Only a St. Bernard can tell whether the snow which has drifted during the night is strong enough to bear the weight of a man, or whether that man would sink beyond rescuing."

Jan and his brother waited respectfully when she stopped speaking and stared at the mountain-tops, until she said, "Sometimes, you will find an ice-bridge. Then you must go very carefully. If it creaks beneath your weight, never let any human being step on it, even if you must fight him back. Your father, Rex, died when an ice-bridge broke through; but he saved four men from death. Always remember one thing. To die doing one's duty is the greatest honor that can come to a St. Bernard."

The two puppies whined softly and their mother knew that each of her children was promising that he would do his best to be worthy of such a father.

"Ah," said Prince Jan to his brother, as their mother crossed the yard toward the kennel, "some day we, too, will go out and do our work. Won't that be glorious, Rollo?"

In their happiness they raced to their mother, who watched them with loving, proud eyes. When they reached her side Jan measured himself to see how much bigger he must grow, for though he was large for his age, he was only six months old.

"Oh, if I could only grow faster, mother!" he cried.

"Be patient, Jan," she answered, biting his ear gently. "Your time is coming soon!"

"My time is coming! My time is coming!" Jan leaped and barked in glee.

"Mine, too!" called Rollo. "We'll work together, Jan!"

The big door leading from the enclosure where the dogs romped and played swung open, and two men who came out, stood looking at the dogs. The puppies watched eagerly, for these men had charge of the youngsters. All the dogs knew them, and even if the men had been strangers the Hospice dogs would have known they were monks who belonged to the Hospice, for the clothes they wore were different from the clothes of other men who came to the Hospice for a day or two.

A long, black, close-fitting coat reached almost to the feet of each monk, a peaked hood hung between his shoulders and a little round, black, skull-cap was on his head. All of the monks dressed the same way, and when it was cold and they went out on the trail, they took off the little cap and pulled the peaked hood over their heads and around their ears.

The dogs hurried to the monks and one of the men leaned down and felt Jan's legs and back. Prince Jan looked anxiously into the two kindly faces. He had seen them do the same thing with other puppies, and afterwards many of his playmates went away and never returned. At first he and Rollo thought they had died on the trail, like their ancestors; but Jan's mother shook her head sadly and said, "They were not strong enough to do the work."

Now he remembered this and wondered if he would be sent away. His little legs and back stiffened so that the monks would see how strong he was.

"I believe this will be one of the best dogs we have had since Barry's time," said Brother Antoine, running his hand along Jan's back. "He has wonderful muscles and a very strong back. We will take him out and give him a trial to-morrow."

Jan licked the hand that rested on his head, then he dashed to his mother's side, yelping with excitement and panting out the good news.

She looked with pride into his happy eyes and said, "You are going to be just like your father! He was a descendant of Barry, the bravest dog of us all. You will be a credit to your ancestors!"

"I will do the very best I can," promised little Prince Jan. Then he lay down and wrinkled his soft forehead as he tried to remember everything that Bruno and his mother had taught him, so that he would be ready for his first lesson.

The next morning he was wide awake before

any of the other dogs. They all slept in a big basement under the Hospice building. Jan could see the arched corridors that reached along the big room with its floor of grey stone. The cows of the Hospice were kept in the basement, too, for there was never any green grass outside for them to graze upon. Here and there curled dogs that Prince Jan knew. Jupitiére, Junon, Mars, Vulcan, Pluton, Leon, and Bruno were not far away from him.

At last the door leading to the yard was opened and the dogs raced and tumbled out, looking like great, tawny lions and cubs rushing from stone cages. They ate a breakfast of boiled rice that was poured into troughs for them, then Jan turned impatiently to the door, hoping it would not be very long before Brother Antoine would come for him. When the monk appeared on the stone steps Jan trembled nervously, and went forward quickly, but stopped at a certain point. He remembered what his mother had told him and Rollo. They must never step beyond that place, even though visitors called to them. Brother Antoine smiled as he saw the pup halt.

"Time for your first lesson, Prince Jan," said

the monk in his gentle voice that all the dogs loved. Rollo whined pleadingly, and the monk laughed, "Yes, you, too, Rollo. Come along, both of you!"

With sharp yelps they followed to the door, through the arched corridors, up a short flight of steps, past a big room. Rollo and Jan waited impatiently while Brother Antoine unfastened three doors, one after the other, and then as the last one opened, the two dogs dashed out into the snow.

They gave little barks of joy and thrust their noses into the cold white mass, tossing it high and digging into drifts with broad clumsy paws, then stopping to rush at each other and tumble almost out of sight in their play.

It was summer-time at the Hospice, though no one would have guessed it, for the snow lay in masses on all sides, the little lake was frozen over, and the peaks of the mountains were sheeted with snow and blue-white ice that never melted the year around. There was not so much danger for travellers during the months of July and August, and as the work was lighter for both the dogs and the monks, the puppies were then taken out for their first lessons.

A collar was fastened to Prince Jan's neck and from it hung a small bell that tinkled clearly with each step the proud little fellow took. When he looked back he saw his brother also had a collar and bell, and then a casket was tied to each pup's neck. Both dogs watched the monks and at a sign from Brother Antoine they trotted carefully along the narrow, slippery way.

There were no trees, grass, or flowers growing for many miles around the Hospice, for the earth was buried deep under rocks, and these rocks were covered all the time with a white blanket of snow, which drifted into the hollow places until it was many feet deep. The narrow trail twisted between cragged mountains, and often the dogs could look down so far that it would have made them dizzy, had they not been Hospice dogs.

They trudged along happily for a long distance, then Brother Antoine spoke to his companion and commanded Jan and Rollo to lie down. They obeyed at once, and watched him go on alone until he disappeared around a bend of the trail. The pups looked at each other anxiously, and fixed their eyes on the face of the monk who had stayed with them, but he was staring at the trail. Prince Jan whimpered softly, and Rollo echoed the sound, but neither of them rose to their feet.

"Wait!" said the monk, and the dogs trembled with eagerness as they sniffed the cold air.

At last the monk ordered, "Go!" Instantly they leaped to their feet and raced along the narrow pathway, their noses close against the snow to catch the scent of Brother Antoine who was somewhere ahead of them.

At times they ran from the path to follow little gullies of heavy snow. They knew that Brother Antoine had trodden here, though no trace of his steps could be seen on the surface, for the snow slid quickly in the summer months, and masses of it kept covering the slopes as it shifted rapidly. In this way Jan and Rollo trailed Brother Antoine until they reached a spot where they could find no further scent though they went around in circles. The other monk, who had followed more slowly, stood watching them as they paused, uncertain what to do. He made no sign to help them, but suddenly Prince Jan gave a sharp bark and thrust his nose deeply into the snow, where he began digging as fast as he could. Rollo, too, understood, and his front paws worked as fast as his brother's until they had uncovered the face and shoulders of Brother Antoine, who had buried himself under the snow to see if they could find him.

Both puppies leaped about in glee, barking and yelping until the sides of the narrow pass sent back echoes like many unseen dogs answering them. Brother Antoine rose to his feet, smiling. He patted the soft, fuzzy heads while the other monk told how the dogs had acted without any help at all.

"Jan led the way," he said to Brother Antoine. "He shows wonderful intelligence."

"It is his father's blood," replied Brother Antoine, then he pointed toward the Hospice. "Go back!" he ordered. Prince Jan started obediently toward his home, while Rollo followed closely, but every once in a while both dogs turned back, or waited a bit, until the monks caught up to them.

They reached the stone steps leading up to the front door of the Hospice. The door swung open, and the puppies, with Brother Antoine, trudged through the long corridor, down to the basement, under the high archways and once again were in the big, enclosed yard. The other dogs crowded about them as they stood proud and important, for that day Prince Jan and Rollo had learned the first lesson on the trail. But they both knew that this was only play and their real work would come when the snow piled so deep about the walls of the Hospice that it almost reached the high, peaked roof.

Chapter II

The Land of Snow

THE lesson of the trail had to be repeated several times, before the two puppies understood just what they were expected to do. Day after day their mother told them more about the brave deeds of the St. Bernard dogs, for the work of the mother-dogs of the Hospice was to teach the puppies to be kindly, obedient and loyal to the trust placed in them by the good monks.

July and August, the two months that were called the summer-time at the Hospice, passed swiftly, and Jan and Rollo knew that very soon it would be winter. The first big snow storm blew over the mountains early in September, while Jan and his brother slept, warm and snug, beside their mother. Next morning no sun could be seen, and when the dogs rushed into the enclosures, dark clouds, shrieking winds, and sheets of driving snow told them that winter had

14

begun and soon there would be hard work for them all.

Jan and Rollo quivered with excitement and envy when they saw the older dogs pass through the long corridors that day, and each time one of the monks came into the basement where the dogs waited, all of them started to their feet and wagged their tails, hoping to be taken out for work.

While Jan and Rollo watched and waited, their mother talked to them.

"Sometimes," she said, "you will find a white mound, and you must never pass it by without digging to see if any one is under it. You have learned already that when you find a man, you must lick his face and hands to waken him, and if you cannot rouse him, so that he will stand up, or put his arms about your neck, you must hurry to the Hospice to bring the monks. That way, you may save a life, and then, perhaps, you will have a collar or a medal, like Barry, and travellers who sit in the big room will be told that you were worthy of your ancestors."

"Tell us about the Big Room," begged Rollo, while Jan gave a gentle little nudge of his nose to coax his mother. Both of them had heard

many times from their mother, from Bruno, and
the other older dogs, about the Big Room, yet
they never tired hearing of it. Now they
bunched themselves into furry balls with their
heads against their mother's soft breast, as she
began: "In the Big Room are many beautiful
pictures that have been sent from travellers rescued by our kinsfolk. Sometimes a handsome
collar is sent to a dog that has saved a life, but
the greatest honor of all was the medal that was
given to Barry, and the beautiful marble monument that you puppies have seen near the Hospice. Your father had a collar sent to him by
the men he saved. They knew he would never
wear it, but they asked that it be hung above the
fireplace in the Big Room. Some day, I hope
you, Jan and Rollo, will have collars there.
Now, run and play," she ended, giving each pup
a push with her nose. "Even though you cannot
go out to-day, you must romp, for that will make
your backs and legs strong. If you are not
strong you will be sent away from the Hospice
and never come back. That is a terrible thing
for a St. Bernard. I don't want it to happen to
either of you!"

Though it was so cold and stormy, the two

dogs leaped to their feet and ran through the half-shut door that led to the big enclosure. Jan was ahead, and Rollo scampered after him. Around and around the yard they went, dodging each other until Rollo managed to catch the tip of his brother's fuzzy tail. This did not make Jan stop running, so Rollo was dragged after him through the heaps of snow, rolling over and over but clinging tightly until Jan turned and pounced upon him. They tumbled about, sometimes Jan was on top, sometimes Rollo, and they looked like a huge, yellow spider with eight sturdy, furry legs kicking wildly. At last, panting, they sprawled facing each other with pink tongues hanging from their open mouths and eyes twinkling merrily.

The sound of Brother Antoine's voice made them look up quickly, and they saw two visitors were with him. The dogs were accustomed to visitors, for in the summer many people came to see the Hospice and the dogs, but in the winter the strangers sought refuge from storms.

"Come on, Rollo," called Jan, as the monk and the men with him came down the steps. "There's Brother Antoine. I'll beat you to him! Show him how fast we can run!"

Before Jan had finished, the two puppies were
tearing madly toward the monk and the other
men. One of these strangers wore a long fur
overcoat, the other was a much younger man
with kindly grey eyes. Jan won the race, but
was going so fast that he could not stop until he
bumped against this grey-eyed man, who smiled
and leaned down to pat him. Jan squirmed
around and touched the hand with his nose, then
edged nearer Brother Antoine, who called the
dogs about him.

It was a splendid sight to see them cross
the enclosure, their great heads held proudly,
their eyes beaming with intelligence and kindness, the strong muscles moving beneath the
tawny skins, as though each one of them, old
and young, understood that the honor of his forefathers must be guarded from any act that would
injure it.

Bruno limped slowly, Jan's mother walked
sedately beside him, back of them were Jupitiére,
Junon, Mars, Vulcan, Pluton, Leon, and among
the older dogs came those the same age as Jan
and Rollo, followed by the mothers with still
smaller puppies. They reached a place in the
yard where all of them stopped, and though the

man in the fur coat, who stood a distance back of Brother Antoine and the younger man, called to them, the dogs only wagged their tails and did not go any closer.

"You will have to come further," said the monk. "The dogs know that they must not cross to you, for the first thing a puppy learns is to respect the boundary line."

The fur-coated man moved to where Brother Antoine and the other man stood, then the dogs grouped about while the monk talked to the visitors.

"They seem to understand every word you say," the old man spoke. "Their eyes are so intelligent."

"They are living sermons on obedience, loyalty, and self-sacrifice," answered Brother Antoine's gentle voice. "Not one of these dogs would hesitate to risk his life to save his most bitter enemy. That has been their heritage for almost a thousand years, now."

"Natural instinct counts for a great deal," the grey-eyed man spoke as he looked into the upturned faces of the dogs, "but the patient training you give them has developed it."

"The older dogs help us teach the youngsters,"

went on the monk, whose hand rested on Jan's head. "We send out four dogs each morning— two younger ones and two of the old ones. One pair goes on the trail down the Italian slope toward Aosta, the other travels the Swiss path leading to Martigny. None of them turns back until the last cabin of refuge has been reached, where they look to see if any person is waiting. It is not unusual for the dogs to stay out all night in a hard storm. There have been many instances of their remaining away for two days and nights, without food or shelter, though at any time they could have come home."

"Our guide showed us the cabin," interrupted the older man. "The footprints of the dogs proved they had been there a short time before us. We followed their tracks until the storm covered them. It was a lucky thing the storm did not break earlier."

"The dogs would have found you, Mr. Pixley," the monk replied. "You see, since we have had a telephone from the Hospice, each time travellers start up the trails, we know when they leave Martigny or Aosta and how many are on the way. If they do not reach here in reasonable time, or a storm breaks, we send out the dogs at once. It was much harder in the other days, before we had telephones, for we could not tell how many poor souls were struggling in the snow. The dogs seemed to understand, too, and so they kept on searching until they believed they had found all."

"I would not have attempted this trip had I not been assured that it was too early for a bad storm," said Mr. Pixley. "It is foolhardy, not courageous, to face these mountains in a winter storm. I cannot imagine any one being so rash as to try it, but I suppose many do?"

"During the winter only poor peasants travel the Pass," was Brother Antoine's answer. "They cross from Italy to seek work in the vineyards of France or Switzerland for the summer. When summer is over they return home this way, because it would mean a long and expensive trip by rail, which would take all they have earned for a whole year. An entire family will travel together, and often the youngest will be a babe in its mother's arms."

"I should think they would wait till later in the summer, and take no risks."

"Only the good God knows when a snow storm will overtake one in the Pass of Great St.

Bernard," Brother Antoine said. "Even in our summer months, when a light shower of rain falls in the Valley below, it becomes a heavy snow up here, and many people are taken unawares. After winter really begins, in September, the snow is often from seven to ten feet deep and the drifts pile up against the walls of the Hospice as high as the third story roof."

"I had planned to visit Berne," Mr. Pixley spoke now, "but after this sample of your winter weather I have decided to return home to California. I do not enjoy snow storms. We have none where I live, you know."

Brother Antoine nodded. "Yes, I know; but I hope some day you will visit Berne and see Barry. His skin was mounted and is kept in the Museum at Berne. You know his record? He saved forty-two people and died in 1815, just after the terrible storm that cost the lives of almost all the Hospice dogs. Only three St. Bernards lived through those days—Barry, Pluto, and Pallas. A few crawled home to die of exhaustion and cold; the rest lie buried under thousands of feet of snow, but they all died like heroes!"

"A glorious record!" exclaimed the younger

man, who had been patting Jan while the others talked. "I remember, when I was a very small boy, that I found a picture in a book. It showed a St. Bernard dog digging a man from the snow, and last night I recognized the picture in that painting which hangs over the fireplace in the refectory."

"It was a gift from a noted artist," replied the monk. "The dogs used to carry a little saddle with a warm shawl, but the extra weight was hard on them, so we do not use the saddle any longer, but a flagon, or wooden keg of white brandy that we call 'kirsch,' is fastened to the collar, together with a bell, so that the tinkling will tell that help is near, even though it may be too dark for any one to see the dog."

"I notice that most of the dogs are short-haired," the grey-eyed man observed. "Such fur as this pup's would afford better protection against the cold. He has a magnificent coat of hair!"

"That is the only point against him," said Brother Antoine. "During the big storm of 1815 we learned that long-haired dogs break down from the snow clinging and freezing like a coat of mail; or the thick hair holding moisture developed pneumonia. We brought Newfoundland dogs to fill the kennels when only three St. Bernards were left, but the long, heavy hair of the new breed that was part Newfoundland and part St. Bernard proved a failure. They could not stand the snow storms. Now, we very rarely keep a long-haired pup. He is generally sold or presented to some one who will give him kind treatment."

Jan looked suddenly at Rollo and the other puppies near him. All except himself had short hair. Now he remembered his mother's worried eyes each time the monks had examined him. He hurried to her side and pushed her with his nose, as he whispered, "Mother, will they send me away because I have long hair? You know, Brother Antoine said that I was one of the best dogs they have had for a long time!"

"Don't worry, Jan," she soothed him. "Even though your fur is long, you are so strong and so like your father, who had long hair, too, that I am sure you will be kept here. Hurry, Jan! Brother Antoine is calling you back."

Jan pushed among the other dogs until he stood again at the monk's side. The two strangers looked at Jan, and Brother Antoine touched the pup's head lovingly.

"His father was one of our best dogs," the monk spoke. "But that was not surprising. He was a direct descendant of Barry. Four travellers owe their lives to Jan's father, Rex."

The little fellow tried not to look too proud as he listened again to the story his mother had told him and Rollo many times.

"Rex was guiding four men to the Hospice after a big storm last Fall. It was the worst since 1815. The men told us the story after they reached us. They had lost all hope, their guide had fallen down a crevasse and they were exhausted when Rex found them. They knew that their only chance of life was to follow him. He went ahead, moving very slowly and looking back while he barked to encourage them. An ice-bridge had formed. It was hidden by deep snow and they did not understand the danger that Rex knew so well. The dog went ahead, the men keeping closely behind him. Half way across he turned and began barking fiercely, and as they drew nearer, he started toward them uttering savage snarls.

"They thought the dog had gone mad, and

backed away as he advanced threateningly. Then suddenly his snarl turned to a mournful howl that was lost in frightful cracking as the ice-bridge broke away. Rex was never seen again, but his warning prevented those four men from being smothered in the chasm under hundreds of feet of snow. So, you see, this little fellow comes of royal blood. That is why we named him 'Prince Jan.' He looks just like his father, too!"

Jan thrust his warm nose into Brother Antoine's hand.

"I want to be like my father and Barry," he said, hoping they would understand him, as he understood them. "I will do my very best to be worthy of them both!"

The visitors and the monk did not know what Jan said, but the other dogs understood. Bruno's dim eyes beamed on the pup.

"You will be a credit to us all, Prince Jan!"

The strangers and Brother Antoine left the yard, and the dogs formed in little groups to talk among themselves, as they always did when new people came to see them.

"That man came from America," Bruno said to Jan's mother.

"Lots of people from America visit us," she replied, trying not to yawn, for the storm had kept her awake. All night, while she felt the warm little bodies of the puppies pressed against her side, she had stared into the darkness, thinking of the time when Prince Jan and his brother must go out, like their father, Rex, to do the work of the St. Bernards.

"Yes," Bruno added in a queer voice, "but this man said he was from California, where they never have any snow!"

"What?" shouted all the dogs together. "A place where they never have any snow? Oh, what a funny place that must be!"

"What do they walk on?" asked Jan's mother curiously.

Before Bruno could answer, Jan shoved up and said earnestly: "But, mother, how do dogs save people where there is no snow?"

"I am sure I don't know," she told him. "Ask Bruno."

Neither Bruno nor any of the other dogs could explain this mystery, though Jan went to each in turn for an answer to his question. At last he lay down, his nose wedged between his paws, his yellow forehead wrinkled with thought, and he stared across at the tops of the great white peaks above the enclosure until his soft eyes closed in sleep.   Soon he was dreaming that he was digging travellers from the snow and asking them, "Won't you please tell me how a dog can save people in a land where there is no snow?"

But none of them could answer his question.

Chapter III

A New World

THE next morning Mr. Pixley and Brother Antoine returned to the kennel yard and Jan wagged his tail politely to show that he recognized the visitor, who leaned down and patted him while talking to the monk.

"You may be sure he will receive the very best care," said the man from California.

"We are always treated kindly," Prince Jan hastened to say, and he glanced at Rollo, who replied, "Of course, we are!"

The two pups did not notice Mr. Pixley's next words, "My little girl will be delighted with him."

Brother Antoine called, "Here, Jan," and when the little fellow stood looking up with bright, expectant eyes, the monk fastened a collar about the dog's neck.

Jan trembled. He was sure that he was now

going to be sent out to do his first work on the trail. It would not be playing this time, but real work like the big dogs. The collar was stiff but he did not mind the discomfort, for it meant that he was not a puppy any longer. He twisted his head to see which of the older dogs was to go out with him, as he crossed the forbidden line with the monk. The only dog that followed Jan was his brother, Rollo, and when Brother Antoine ordered, "Go back, Rollo!" the pup's ears and tail drooped and he slunk back to his mother as though in disgrace.

"The big dogs must be waiting outside," thought Jan happily, and he walked proudly beside the monk until he stood on the top step, then he looked back at his mother, Bruno, Rollo, and the other dogs who were watching him. Usually they all barked joyously when a pup was to go out on his first real work, and the noisy barks were advice. Now, the only sounds were two short barks from Bruno, "Goodbye, Jan! Remember your father!"

"I will remember him!" he called back, and then he wondered at the long, despairing howl from his mother. It filled his heart with dread.

"Come, Jan," the monk spoke, and the little
fellow turned obediently toward the door that
would shut him from sight of the other dogs.
His feet dragged now, and as he passed through
the doorway leading to the long corridor he
looked back once more.

When he stood outside the big entrance door,
he saw the snow covering the mountains and
hiding the chasms that he had seen in the summer
when he had been out having his lessons with
Rollo. He knew these smooth, level places held
real danger. Then he saw dog tracks leading in
two directions from the steps, but none of the
older dogs were waiting for him. As he looked
up with questioning, brown eyes, Brother Antoine leaned down and fastened a stout rope to
the new collar and handed the end of this rope
to Mr. Pixley, who was muffled in his big, fur
coat. A guide was with Mr. Pixley. As they
stood there a moment, the door of the Hospice
again opened, and this time the grey-eyed man
and another guide came out. The kind, grey
eyes looked at Jan, then the man stooped over
and patted him gently, and no one but the dog
heard the pitying voice that said, "Poor little
Prince Jan! Good-bye!"

Brother Antoine lifted Jan's nose and the pup looked into the monk's eyes, but there was something he did not understand. It was all so different from what the other dogs had told him. He felt the rope tug his collar and knew that he must follow this stranger. He heard again a heart-rending howl from his mother, "Good-bye, Jan, good-bye!" Bruno's voice blended with hers, and then the voices of all the dogs Jan knew and loved mingled in that call. Something hurt him all over, but most of the hurt was in his heart.

He halted suddenly, pulled stiffly on the rope and the wild cry he sent in response echoed mournfully from the high, white crags and died away to a whispering moan, as Prince Jan, with low-hanging head and drooping tail, travelled down the path that his ancestors had trodden many years on their errands of mercy. He wondered why he had been sent out with a rope tied to his collar, why no older dog went with him, and why he must follow this stranger instead of one of the monks. Jan felt that he was disgraced. Someway he had failed. For a while he followed despondently, then he tried to comfort himself as he trudged at the end of the rope.

"Bruno and mother will know what is the matter," he thought hopefully. "I'll ask them as soon as I get home to-night."

He looked back wistfully several times to see if the kindly, grey-eyed stranger might be following them, but he had taken the opposite trail from the one Mr. Pixley was travelling. Jan did not mind the long tramp which ended at a place where houses were scattered about. Here a carriage and horses were brought, and Jan would have been much interested in these strange things had he not been so worried. He felt himself lifted into the carriage with Mr. Pixley; then, as it moved, Jan was thrown against the fur coat and looked up in fright.

"You are going to a new land," Mr. Pixley said, smoothing the pup's velvety ear.

The dog lifted one paw and laid it on the man's knee, the brown eyes that looked up were dull with misery. Jan knew, now, that he was being taken away from the Hospice.

"Won't you take me back?" he begged.

But the man only heard a little whimper, and gave the dog a quick pat. "You and Elizabeth will be great friends. Lie down now and be quiet!"

Jan dropped to the floor of the carriage, his head between his paws, and his eyes that stared at the strange new master were full of wistful pleading.

After that ride came days in a big, dark place that bumped and jerked with horrible noises. He did not know that he was on a train. Jan had lived all his life where the only disturbing sounds were the soft thud of melting snow and the hissing of the avalanches down the mountain sides. These strange noises hurt his ears. The pain in his heart kept growing until he could only lie still and draw his breath in smothered little whimpers that tore the inside of his throat. He could not eat nor drink.

When Mr. Pixley took him from the train, the dog was led through crowds of people and bustling, noisy streets that made Jan cringe and cower. At last they reached a place where water stretched so far that it touched the sky, and the water kept moving all the time. This frightened him, for he had never seen any water excepting in the little lake at the Hospice, and that water did not move, for it was nearly always frozen over. Bewildered, Jan hung back, but the man to whom Mr. Pixley had handed the rope dragged the dog up a walk of boards to a strange-looking house on top of the water. Jan stumbled down the dark stairs, into a hot, smelly place where he was fastened to a wall. An old sack was thrown down, water and meat placed before him, then he was left alone. Whistles screamed, bells jangled, all sorts of noises pounded Jan's shrink ing, sensitive ears as he cowered in an agony of fear. The boat moved; but he thought, as it puffed and trembled, that a huge, strange animal had swallowed him alive.

The rolling motion made him very sick. He could neither eat nor sleep, but grew stiff and sore during the days and nights he was kept tied in the hold of the vessel. Homesick and lonesome, poor little Prince Jan lay for hours crying softly, but the only attention any one gave him was to fill pans with water and food.

One day two women, wearing white caps on their heads, climbed down the stairs with a little girl and boy. The children ran and put their arms about the dog's neck and Jan wriggled and squirmed with happiness, while he licked their hands and faces.

"Don't touch him," cried one of the women,

pulling the girl away. "He is filthy, beside, he might bite you."

The child drew back in alarm. Jan's gentle eyes watched them and his tail waved slowly, trying to make them know that he loved them and would not hurt them or anybody in the world.

"He won't hurt us, Nurse," the boy declared and put his hand on the dog's big head. "I don't care whether he's dirty or clean, he's a bully fine dog, and I wish he belonged to me and sister!"

"Oh, if they will only stay with me!" hoped Jan. "Maybe they would understand and some day take me back to the Hospice."

The boy smiled into Jan's eyes, but he did not know what the dog was trying to say.

"Come, children, we must go," one of the women spoke. "Now, you have seen a dog that cost over a thousand dollars and is being taken to live in California, where oranges grow and there is never any snow."

Jan turned quickly. He remembered all the dogs at the Hospice had talked about the place where there was never any snow.

"How can a dog save lives where there is no

snow?" he asked; but the women and children, as they turned away, thought he was whining because they were leaving him alone.

With miserable eyes Jan lay staring into the dark, wondering how he could be like his father and Barry in a country where there was no snow.

Chapter IV

THE LAND OF NO SNOW

THE voyage ended, then followed another long trip in a train and Jan reached his new home. A little girl with long, yellow curls, big blue eyes, and pink cheeks, danced down the steps from the wide porch of a big house as they approached.

Mr. Pixley caught her in his arms, then put her on the ground and called to Jan, who was still in the automobile which had met them at the station. The dog leaped out and ran to the child, looking into her face, while his tail bobbed and waved.

"Oh, you beautiful Prince Jan!" she cried, throwing her arms about his neck and squeezing him tightly. "I love you!"

Jan's tongue caressed her hands, touched her cheek, and his body squirmed and twisted, then he flopped on the ground and rolled on his back, waving his paws to show that he loved her.

Obeying her call, he trotted beside her, past strange trees growing on stretches of fresh, green grass. Jan looked about him and saw that this new stuff that was so soft when he walked upon it, reached down to the blue water, and that water sparkled as far as he could see, and then it seemed to become a part of the sky. Wonderful things that gave out delicate perfume formed brilliant patches about the house and even clung high up on the walls. Later, he learned these things were flowers, and when the wind blew softly, they bent and swayed like lovely ladies in their prettiest gowns, bowing and dancing. From the thick leaves of the trees floated songs of hidden birds. Jan's head turned quickly from side to side, trying to see everything and understand what he saw, but the most wonderful thing to him was the dear little mistress, who talked to him as if she knew he understood her words.

All the people in the big house were very kind to Jan, and he soon grew accustomed to his new home. His only duty was to take care of Elizabeth, who was so gentle and loving that he was glad and proud to guard her. Wherever she went, he went, too.

The governess heard Elizabeth's lessons out
on the lawn under the shade of an orange tree,
and Jan kept close at hand, watching the little
girl's face, and waiting patiently for the lesson
to end.   Then a pony was led to the front door,
and as Elizabeth rode over the firm sand of the
beach, Jan raced beside her, barking or rushing
out to fight back a wave that was sneaking too
close.   He loved the water, and the best time
of all, he thought, was when his mistress took
her swimming lesson and he could plough
through the waves beside her.   Often she would
lie on her back in the hissing, white surf, holding to Jan's collar until they both landed on the
warm sand.   Sometimes the two of them would
dig a big hole, and the dog would scrunch into
it, while she buried him until only his nose and
eyes could be seen.   Jan was so happy that at
times he forgot the Hospice and the work his
mother had told him he must do.   When he did
remember it, he would puzzle over and over,
"But, how can I save people's lives here, where
there is never any snow, and every one is happy
and safe?"

Christmas came, and there was a glittering
tree with lights and beautiful things on it.   All

the family patted Jan when Elizabeth took down
a handsome collar.

"This is for you, Jan," she said.

As she fastened it about his neck, he thought
of the big room at the Hospice, but he knew,
now, no collar of his would ever hang there.
Suddenly, all the old longing for the Hospice
dogs and the work made him walk slowly out of
the house and lie down on the front porch, where
he could see the blue ocean dancing in the warm
sunshine, the soft, green grass, and the beautiful
flowers.

"Oh, if I could only go back home to the
snow and do my work there!" he wished, and
then, in a little while he fell sound asleep.

The Fairy of Happy Dreams was very busy
that Christmas Day, and when she flew over
Prince Jan and saw he was so lonesome and
homesick, she touched him with her magic wand
and fluttered away, smiling.

And Prince Jan dreamed he was at the door
of the Hospice. The little wooden keg hung
from his collar. Rollo, with another collar and
keg, romped beside him, pulling playfully at
Jan's hairy neck, while Brother Antoine and
other monks stood on the upper step, smiling

and saying, "He is just like his father, and Rex was descended from Barry! Prince Jan is of royal blood. He will be a credit to his ancestors!"

In the dream, Jan bounded away through the crisp, biting air, his big paws sinking in the cold, fluffy snow. Oh, how good it felt!

"My time has come! My time has come!" he shouted as he leaped with joy.

"Jan! Jan! Remember your father!" his mother and Bruno called after him.

"I will," he answered. Then he and Rollo raced down the slippery path, their voices, like deep-sounding bells, giving forth the cry of the St. Bernards. They trod over ice-bridges, ploughed through deep drifts, sliding and floundering, following the trail of their forefathers, and sniffing as they ran.

Suddenly Jan stopped and thrust his nose into a deep drift. Then he and Rollo dug furiously, until Jan cried, "Run, Rollo, run to the Hospice!"

Rollo whirled and disappeared, while Jan's rough tongue licked the snow until he saw the round, soft face of a child, and beneath that child lay its mother. Both were very quiet.

Jan licked their faces, he pushed them with his nose to rouse them, then he crowded his warm body closely against them, and his eyes watched the trail. Soon he gave a wild yelp, for he saw Rollo coming and back of him hurried Brother Antoine and one of the men of the Hospice who helped on the trail.

The men lifted the woman and child, and wrapped them in warm shawls, then they unfastened the keg from Jan's collar, and as the woman opened her eyes they made her drink the liquid. Some of it was given to the child. Brother Antoine carried the little one in his arms while the other man held the woman, and Jan and Rollo trotted ahead of them to beat down the snow and make the path easier to travel. Bruno and the other dogs in the kennel yard sent back answering calls to Jan and Rollo. The door opened and kindly hands received the woman and child, and carried them to shelter and warmth.

Brother Antoine stooped and patted Jan's head, and brushed off snow that still clung to the long hair on the dog's back, saying very softly, "The Blessed Mother guided you, Jan; for you have saved a mother and child on Christmas Day!"

Then he heard laughter and voices saying, "Jan is dreaming again! Wake up, Jan!"

He woke to see waving palms, green grass, flowers, and the warm sunshine of a land where there is never any snow. His heart, which had been throbbing madly with joy, grew sad. He looked at his little mistress and her friends smiling at him so kindly, and wished he could tell them his dream and beg them to send him back where he could be useful and do the work of his father and Barry.

But the talk of dogs is different from ours; even people who speak the same language often misunderstand one another. Once in a great while some person is wise enough and good enough to understand what dogs try to say, but Prince Jan's little mistress, though she loved him dearly, never knew what was in his heart.

The months slipped away until Jan was fully grown. His tawny-red and white hair was as soft as silk, and when he put his paws on a man's shoulders, their eyes were the same height. In spite of his strength and size, he was gentle and kind. Every one loved him and he loved everybody.

The only sadness in his life was in knowing that he could not help people in a place where there was no snow. One night, as he came on the porch, Jan thought it was snowing, and he raced to the spot where he had seen the flakes falling in the bright moonlight; but when he pushed his nose into the white glistening things beneath a tree, he found they were only petals from the orange blossoms, the perfumed snow-flakes of California, and Jan lay down among them, the old longing for his home and his work tugging at his heart.

Chapter V

JAN LEARNS TO HATE

FOUR happy years passed by. Elizabeth had grown into a beautiful young lady, but she loved Jan as much as ever, and he was always at her side.

Then one morning when Jan, as usual, went to the front porch to tell Mr. Pixley that breakfast was ready, there was no one sitting in the rocker where Jan expected to find his master reading the paper, and no kindly voice called, "All right, Jan! Tell them I'm coming!"

Slowly the dog went back to the big diningroom. But Elizabeth and her mother were not in their accustomed places, either. Puzzled, he trotted through the hallway and up the wide stairs, following the sound of murmuring voices in Mr. Pixley's room. Through the half-open door Jan saw two strange men talking to Elizabeth and her mother. On the bed, very white and quiet, Mr. Pixley was lying.

46

"The only chance is an operation by Dr. Corey of London," one of the men spoke to Mrs. Pixley, and the other man nodded.

"We can cable to London and have him sail immediately for New York, while we are on our way from here," added the second man to Elizabeth, who was watching them very anxiously.

"Do you think my father can stand the trip?" she asked.

"It would be less dangerous than losing time for Dr. Corey to come to California after he reaches New York," both doctors declared.

Jan saw that Elizabeth's eyes were full of tears and he slipped softly to her and pushed his nose into her hand. She glanced down and tried to smile at him, but her lips trembled and she hurried to her room. Mrs. Pixley followed her, and when Jan found them, Elizabeth was crying in her mother's arms, while Mrs. Pixley, whose own face was wet with tears, tried to comfort her. After awhile they began talking in low tones, and Jan edged between their closely-drawn chairs, wishing very hard that he could understand what it all meant. He would have been as much worried as they were, had he known that Mr. Pixley's life could only be saved by the

famous surgeon from England, and that even if
the operation were successful it would mean that
Elizabeth and her parents would have to be away
from home many months. But Jan was only
a dog, so their words meant nothing to him.

After that hour everything was in confusion.
Servants hurried about, trunks were dragged
into Elizabeth's room, and clothes were carried
from closets and packed into the empty trunks.
Every once in a while Jan would look down into
a trunk, then watch Elizabeth with his puzzled
eyes.

She saw his worried look and paused in her
packing to pet him, then suddenly she turned
to her mother and said, "Oh, mother! What
about Jan?"

"It will be impossible to take him with us,
for we will have to stay in a hotel, and that would
be hard on Jan, and an additional care for us,
dear. Then, we may have to go to London as
soon as your father is able to travel after the
operation. Dr. Corey could not stay in New
York so long."

"I suppose the servants will be kind to Jan,"
went on Jan's mistress, "but I would feel better

if old John and Mary were still here. They loved Jan and he loved them."

"These new servants seem to be all right," replied Mrs. Pixley. "They know how fond we are of Jan, and I will ask them to be kind to him."

"He's such a dear old fellow, and never makes any trouble, and I don't believe any one could help loving him!" exclaimed Elizabeth, catching the dog's long, silky ears and pulling them gently while his eyes, shining with devotion, looked into her own.

Before noon the next day the trunks had been strapped and taken away. Then Jan saw Mr. Pixley lifted into the automobile where Mrs. Pixley was arranging pillows. Elizabeth came slowly down the steps of the porch with Jan at her side. Then she stooped and took his head between her hands and gazed intently at him.

"Good-bye, Jan! I'll come back again!"

That was what she always said when she was going away for a short time; so Jan wagged his tail and touched her pink cheek with the tip of his tongue. He watched the automobile turn among the orange trees that bordered the winding driveway and waited for a last glimpse of it through the trees. He knew that Elizabeth would turn and call to him when she reached that point.

His ears cocked up and his eyes were bright as the machine came into sight. Then he saw his dear mistress look back at him, her hand waved and her voice called, "Good-bye, Prince Jan! Be a good dog!"

"Woof! Woof!" he answered, as he always answered her "good-bye" call. Then the automobile vanished among the trees.

It was summer time and the middle of the day was very warm, so Jan decided he would take a swim in the ocean. It was great sport battling the huge waves while white sea-gulls darted screaming over his head, fearing he would steal the fish they hoped to catch and eat. Cooled by the water, he returned to the front porch and stretched out where he could see the road, for he always ran and welcomed his folks when they came home from their drives. He was very happy and comfortable until the new housekeeper came out with a broom.

"Get off, you dirty beast!" she cried, shaking the broom over his head. "This porch was washed to-day."

Jan jumped up in surprise. No one had ever spoken to him that way. The old housekeeper, who had gone away, had been his friend. Whenever the family was absent at night Jan had kept her company in her room, and she always had cookies there for him. John, her husband, had been the old stableman.

The broom waved nearer. He looked into the woman's angry face, then walked down the front steps.

"I'll go to the stable till Elizabeth comes home," he thought as he went toward the back of the house.

But, John, the stableman, who had cared for the handsome horses of the Pixleys until automobiles filled the carriage house, had gone away to another place where people still used horses. John had been Jan's loyal friend. The new man, William Leavitt, had not made friends with Jan, but there were many nice dark places, out of William's sight, where Jan often took a nap during the heat of the day, and William never knew it.

Jan was making for a favorite spot under the old family carriage, when William saw him.

"Get out!" he shouted furiously.

The dog stopped. William came closer and lifting his hand, threw a monkey-wrench at Jan. It missed him, and the dog hurried away to the garden, where many trees made dense shadows. There was a spot under a low-hanging pepper tree where Jan dug into the cool, moist earth until he had made a nice, big hole. Then he lay down and uttered a sigh of content. His eyes closed and soon he was sound asleep.

A vicious kick wakened him, and he leaped to his feet to see the gardener standing over him swearing. Jan ran away, but stood a short distance off, watching the man fill up the hole under the tree. As the man finished the work, he saw the dog and hurled a stone which struck above Jan's eye, making a jagged cut that started to bleed.

Half-mad with pain, Jan ran until he found a place in the orange grove, far back from the house, and trembling, he huddled down. His heart thumped and again he suffered from the fear of things he did not understand just as he had felt when his mother howled on the day he had been led from the Hospice.

"If only Elizabeth will come back soon," he

thought, "everything will be right again, and the servants won't be cross to me any more."

The excitement of abuse for the first time in his life and the pain from the wounded eye, which was swollen shut, made him feverish, but he kept hidden all day, suffering from thirst rather than risk further ill-treatment, and all the time he was listening for the sound of wheels and the voice of Elizabeth calling him.

The sun went down, but the family had not come home. Then it grew very quiet and dark, and Jan crawled to the back of the house for food and water, which were always put there at sunset for him. He crept like a thief, ready to rush back to the orange grove if he heard a step approaching.

Both pans were in the accustomed place, but he found them empty. His tongue was so dry and hot that he licked each pan in turn. Then he went around to the front of the house and put his nose to a water faucet, licking it for a drop of moisture. The pipe was dry. Jan looked out at the ocean, over which the moon shone silvery bright, the water sparkled, but he knew he could not drink salt water, and even to look at it now made him more thirsty. At last, unable to resist any longer, he went to the beach and lapped the stinging water that burnt his throat. Then he plunged into the surf and swam out a short distance. But the waves washed over his head and the salt in the wound made him cry with pain, until he reached the shore and dashed back to the orange grove, where he lay moaning pitifully.

His thirst grew worse. Jan rose to his feet, hoping the stable door might be open, as sometimes he had seen it on warm nights, and there was a water trough that always had water in it, for Elizabeth still rode horseback, though the family used the automobiles. The door was closed, so he went back to his hiding-place.

In the morning, almost crazed by thirst, Jan again sought the stable. Drawing near, he heard water running, and, thinking of nothing else, he rushed to the trough where cool, sparkling water flowed from the faucet. William was there, too, but the dog rose on his hind legs and thrust his dry tongue into the water, lapping it in big gulps.

"Get out of that!" he heard William order.

Jan kept on drinking greedily. Then he felt a sharp slash from a carriage whip. He did not

lift his head. Nothing could drive him from
the water. The whip struck hard and fast across
his back, each cut making him shrink, but he
kept on drinking until his terrible thirst had been
quenched. Then he dropped his paws from the
edge of the trough to the floor and turned his
great head, one eye closed, the other bloodshot
and glaring hate and defiance, while his teeth
gleamed and an ugly snarl rumbled in his throat.

A young fellow who was a stranger to Jan
came from the back of the building. The dog
looked at him, then at William, ready to fight
them both. As Jan started toward them, William moved back. Jan growled.

"Do you think he's gone mad, Shorty?" asked
William uneasily.

Jan did not know what the words meant, but
he saw that the man was afraid of him for some
reason. He gave a fierce snarl and faced them.

"Wouldn't drink water if he was mad," replied Shorty. "Why didn't you let him alone,
anyhow? He wasn't bothering you till you hit
him."

"I hate dogs, and you know it," retorted William angrily. "It made me sick to see the Pixleys such fools over this one. We all had to

stand around and wait on that dog as if he was the King of England. I guess he finds out the difference now that the family has gone."

Shorty moved slowly toward Jan, holding out a hand and saying, "You're all right, old fellow!"

But the dog backed off and his nose twitched warningly. He would fight if these men bothered him. With a final growl of defiance Jan left the stable, but he carried with him a new sense of power. He could make people let him alone if he snarled and showed his teeth.

That night he prowled around until he found the garbage cans. So he learned to hide in the daytime and forage like a wild animal at night. If he passed one of the servants, he growled and braced himself stiffly, while his hair rose in a ridge along his back. One glance at his bloodshot eyes and big, white teeth was enough to make every one, man, woman or child, hurry out of his way.

In the excitement of packing for the trip, Elizabeth had neglected to have Jan's hair clipped. Maybe she told the servants to have it cut. Now, the long fur heated and worried the dog constantly and the fleas nearly drove him mad. Day and night, he bit and scratched, tearing out tufts of matted hair until raw, bleeding spots made his body a mass of sores. Each day he grew more savage. He hated every one now; the monks who had sold him, Mr. Pixley who had taken him from the Hospice, Miss Elizabeth who had deserted him, and the servants who abused him.

"I wish I could tell the dogs at the Hospice not to help people who are lost," he thought as he lay in the dark. "If William were lost in the snow and I found him, I would fasten my teeth in his throat."

So, the gentle Prince Jan, whose heart had been full of love and trust, and who wanted to help every one, became a savage beast, ready to fight all people and hating even those whom he once had loved and for whom he would have died gladly.

Chapter VI

THE POUND

SIX months went by and the Pixleys had
not returned, but Jan did not know that
Mr. Pixley was still very ill. The dog
hid or skulked if he met any person, and his
deep growls and twitching nose were so threatening that no one dared to go nearer. His silky
hair was rough and ragged, raw bleeding spots
scarred his body, his eyes were bloodshot and
his tail was almost bare of the long hair that had
once made it a beautiful plume.

His only refuge was the orange grove, where
he spent the days sleeping or licking the bones
he stole from garbage pails, for no one ever
thought to put food or water where he could find
it. The servants feared and hated him, and he
hated them but did not fear them. He knew
his own strength. If any one threatened to
abuse him, Jan was ready to leap and use his
sharp teeth, but so long as people let him alone,
he would not fight.

Late one afternoon, he saw William and a kindly-looking old man with a long, white beard, talking together. They were watching Jan, as the dog lay quietly in the hole that was now his only home; his eyes rolled but he did not lift his head as they came closer.

"He has no use for me," said William, giving a rope to the other man. "Maybe you can handle him alone, but I don't believe it. He's as big and strong as a lion."

William pulled a paper from his pocket and held it to the older man, saying, "Here's a letter from Miss Elizabeth Pixley; you can see what she says. I wrote her about Jan and asked what we should do with him."

The name of Elizabeth caused Jan's ears to prick up and the fierce light in his eyes faded. The strange man came close to the dog and spoke gently. Jan wagged his tail slightly, but kept his eyes on the old man's face.

"You had better look out," warned William. "He can't be trusted a minute."

Jan glared at the stableman. "I wanted to love and help people, not hurt them, until you made me fight," he growled.

"Look out!" cried William. "He's showing

his teeth. He is the worst dog I have ever seen in my life."

The older man studied the dog silently, then smiled and held out his hand. Jan shrank back suspiciously but allowed the hand to touch his back.

"I think I can manage him," said the stranger, then he added, "Come, Jan. Come with me!"

The dog rose to his feet and followed unresistingly down the pathway to the front of the Pixley home, and past the lawn where he had spent so many happy hours, along the firm sand on which he had so often raced beside his mistress's pony in the days gone by. And as he trudged slowly, he kept wondering if she had sent for him. He remembered how Mr. Pixley had led him away from the Hospice at the end of a rope, but at the end of the journey Jan had found Elizabeth and happiness. He lifted his big head and his anxious eyes saw a pitying face as a gentle hand lightly touched his back. It was quite a long walk and the dog was weak from improper food and care. When they entered a little cottage, the old man brought food and water, then sat and watched the dog devour them ravenously. After the dish had been emptied of all food, Jan stood wagging his tail to show his gratitude. The old man laughed.

"Why, you're not any more vicious than I am, Prince Jan! But, you're in pretty bad shape."

He did not tie the rope, but let it drop on the floor while he brought a small tin tub full of warm suds, and gently sponged the dog's body. The next thing was cool salve on the painful sores.

Then Jan was ready to follow this kind friend, and though his legs trembled with weakness, he hastened with the old man into a large room with dirt floor. It was late in the afternoon and the light from two small windows left the place in partial darkness, so that Jan, coming into it, could not see anything at first. But, he heard dogs whining and barking all about him. When he grew accustomed to the dim light, the old man had tied him and gone away.

A number of dogs were fastened by short ropes, and all were staring at the big dog. Shrill yapping made Jan turn quickly to see a tiny, dirty dog with long hair that had once been white but now was matted and grimed, straining on its rope and squinting impudently at him.

"Gracious! You're the biggest dog I ever saw!" exclaimed the midget, which was not much larger than a small kitten. "What is your name, and where on earth did you come from?"

Prince Jan answered politely, then asked, "Is this the kennel where they train dogs to help people in the Land of No Snow?"

"You must be crazy! This is the pound!" snapped the tiny creature, thinking Jan was making fun of it.

"The pound?" echoed Prince Jan. "What is that?"

"Silly! You haven't much sense, even if you are so big! If the dog-catchers get us they bring us to the pound, and if our folks don't come for us pretty soon, we are all shot!"

Several dogs howled in despair, but the snippy little animal only stretched out for a nap.

"Don't you feel badly, too?" questioned Jan.

"Good gracious, no! I travel around with my folks and we live in hotels, and they make me wear a collar. I manage to get away without my collar, sometimes, and some one always takes me to the pound, and my family come there for me as soon as I am lost. They'll be here for me before long. I've been in lots of pounds."

"'You must be crazy! this is the pound!' snapped the tiny creature.

Without further remarks, the spoiled pet
curled itself into a dirty ball and was fast asleep
when the door opened and two young ladies
rushed in and grabbed up the blinking rascal.
He yawned in the face of the girl who held him;
then, petted and scolded, he was carried away.

With hopeless eyes, Jan watched them pass
through the doorway. He understood now, that
Elizabeth had not sent for him, that nobody
cared what happened to him. He lay down and
shut his eyes and tried to shut his ears to the
misery of the other dogs, but he could not sleep.
Jan kept thinking how he had wanted to do
what was right and how hard he had tried to
remember what his mother had taught him. In
this strange land, with no snow and no work to
do, he had failed; and now, he would die in disgrace after a useless life that meant dishonour
to his father and Barry, and the other dogs who
had lived and died doing their duty as St. Bernards.

Through the long hours of the night, though
darkness shut away the sight of the other dogs,
Jan could hear restless movements and choked
whimpers, so that he could not forget where he
was, and at last, when morning broke, he lifted

his head slowly and looked at the dogs around him. Then he remembered that morning at the Hospice when he had wakened early, waiting impatiently for his first lesson on the trail. But these dogs around him, now, were pitiful things, cowering and shivering; the eyes that met his own were dull and hopeless, and the ears all drooped dejectedly.

The dogs started nervously as a key scraped in the lock of the door. Then the old man came into the room and went from one dog to the other, patting each in turn as he placed clean, freshly cooked meat and a pan of water within easy reach. The poor animals shrank back, but as they saw that he did not threaten any of them, the ragged tails flopped and the eyes that followed him were less timid. When he reached Jan, the man stood looking at him and shaking his head slowly. The dog, still suspicious of every human being, bunched his muscles and waited, but the smile and gentle voice, "You poor old fellow! I'm afraid I can't do anything for you," made Jan look up with his great, wistful eyes pleading for sympathy and kindness.

"I'll do the best I can, though," the old man

said, at last, as he untied the rope and turned toward the door.

The dog rose stiffly, for every bone in his gaunt body ached, his legs trembled from weakness due to lack of proper food, but he moved trustingly beside this kindly stranger. As they reached once more the door of the little house where Jan had been washed and fed the night before, the wrinkled hand holding the rope reached out and Prince Jan's hot tongue touched it in a light caress.

Inside the tiny house the man fixed an old comforter then pointing at it, he said, "Go lie down, Jan."

With a sigh that was half-weariness, half gratitude, the dog stretched his tired body on the soft quilt, but his eyes watched every movement of his new friend. Then Jan slept in peace, for the first time since Elizabeth had deserted him.

The odor of warm, fresh meat from a dish near his nose wakened him. As he moved toward it a tiny yellow bird flew across the room and lit on the floor, watching him pertly and edging cautiously to the plate. It paused with head perked impudently on one side and its bright little eyes fixed on the big dog. Jan kept very still, and the old man, sitting across the room, nodded approvingly when the dog allowed the bird to peck at the plate of food. After tasting Jan's dinner, the bird, perched on the edge of the dish, lifted its head and sang as though its throat would burst with music. It finished the song, gave a funny little shake of its wings, then flew across the room and lit on the shoulder of the Poundmaster, where it stayed while he kept moving around the room.

"Go home, Cheepsie," said the old man, and the bird at once darted into a cage hanging at the front window, but the Poundmaster did not shut the cage door.

Then he led Jan to the back porch where the tub of clean soapsuds was ready, and again the dog was washed thoroughly and the salve applied to his sores. Though Jan's heart was almost bursting with gratitude, he could only show it by poking his nose against the kindly hand, or uttering low whimpers.

"I know, old fellow," his new friend said, "you're trying to thank me. It's all right now. Don't worry!"

And Prince Jan knew that it was all right.

That night he slept on the soft comforter in the little house.

As day after day went past, Jan began to feel strong again, but it took eight long months before his beautiful hair grew out and his eyes at last lost their pitiful pleading. At first he could not understand about his new friend, whom he heard other men call "Captain Smith, the poundmaster." He remembered what the little white dog had said about pounds being places where dogs were killed when they had no friends to claim them, but Jan knew that his friend would not hurt any dog.

Each day, now, Jan followed the captain into the long room where dogs were tied with ropes, just as he, himself, had been kept that first night. During sunshiny days of the snowless winter, these dogs were led into the back yard of the bungalow. It had a high board fence, so they could run about and stretch, or lie in the warm grass.

None of these dogs ever stayed very long, but they all soon learned to love the old captain and would rush around his feet or crawl against him, wagging their tails. A few, bolder than the others, leaped up to lick his hands, or pretended

they were going to fight him, but when they got
near, they turned and raced about him in big
circles, barking and yelping as though they were
laughing at the joke.

All the time, the old man stood smiling, his
hands held out to caress those nearest. New
dogs came with the others, and often some of the
older dogs would disappear. Then Prince Jan
would look at the captain, wondering, but never
doubting his friend who loved all dogs.

Chapter VII

Hippity-Hop

THE loving care given Jan by the captain for eight months made him well and happy, and above all brought back his lost faith in people, so that he became the gentle, affectionate dog that he used to be before he knew what cruelty meant.

One of Jan's ancestors had been a Newfoundland dog. These are very large dogs with long, silky black and white hair. Though not so large as the St. Bernards, they resemble them in build and show the same intelligence, loyalty, and kind disposition. Newfoundland dogs are wonderful swimmers and do not have to be trained to go out and rescue people who are drowning. So it was very natural for Prince Jan to enjoy swimming.

The old poundmaster and Jan walked on the beach nearly every day, and if the dog saw a bit of driftwood near the shore, he would swim

out and get it.   His master then put the wood
in a basket so it could be taken home to burn in
the fireplace on cool nights.   Often when Jan
was alone on the beach and spied floating wood,
he dashed through the surf for it, and, if it were
not too heavy, dragged it to the bungalow.
Whenever he did this, he was petted and praised
by the old man.   Then Jan felt very proud because he was helping his master.

One day as he wandered alone on the shore he
saw a lot of wood floating on the waves.   Though
it was quite a distance he did not hesitate to
plunge after it.   The salt water splashed over
his head; sometimes he was completely under
big waves, and once a high curling breaker
caught and turned him over and over, while his
legs stuck up from the peak of the wave, but Jan
thought it all great sport.   He shook his big
head so that his long ears flapped, and his strong
paws sent him into deeper water where the waves
rolled in long lines but did not curl up and break
so roughly as nearer the shore.

The boards were fastened together, and Jan
saw this was a much harder task than he had ever
attempted before.   He grabbed the edge of a
plank in his powerful jaws and twisting sharply,

struck back for land. Several times the force
of the water and the weight of the little raft
made him let go, but each time he caught the
driftwood and fought his way toward the beach.
Land was still quite distant when he heard a
faint noise, and then he saw that a tiny grey kitten was clinging to the boards.

"Hold on," called Jan, but the kitten did not
seem to hear him. It lay perfectly still.

He tried to swim faster, fearing the waves
might wash the little creature off, for at times
the water covered the raft and Jan's head, too.
He gained the shore and dragged the wreckage
far back to safety. Jan sniffed at the kitten.
Its eyes were shut and it did not move. He
knew that most cats are afraid of dogs, so he
went off a little way and sat down, waiting patiently for it to wake up.

After many minutes Jan went over and pushed
it gently with his nose. It did not stir. Then
he sat down and looked at it thoughtfully, remembering that when the dogs of the Hospice
found a traveller in the snow whom they could not
waken, they hurried for help. His mother and
Bruno had told him that, and Jan had never

forgotten those lessons, nor the days he and
Rollo had been trained by Brother Antoine.

His tongue licked the wet fur, but the kitten's
eyes stayed shut. Jan lifted his head, gave a
loud bark and raced away through the sand,
kicking it with his fast-flying feet so that it
formed tiny, yellow clouds.

Into the little sitting-room he rushed, leaving
a damp trail across the floor. The captain
looked up in surprise and stopped lighting his
pipe when the dog, dripping wet, stood in front
of him and barked loudly.

"What's the matter, Jan?" he questioned. "I
never saw you so fussed up! And you're dripping wet, too!"

Jan danced around, barking, then dashed to
the gate but there he stopped and looked back,
wagging his tail.

"Do you want me to go with you?" asked the
old man, rising slowly.

The dog leaped against the gate, shoving it
open, then ran ahead, only to return and bark
again.

"All right," the poundmaster picked up his
cap, and when he followed, Jan's delight could
not have been misunderstood by any one.

"Woof! Woof!" he kept shouting back, and in dog-talk that meant, "Hurry! Hurry!"

And Captain Smith did hurry as fast as he could, but Jan reached the driftwood long before the old man. The kitten was in the same place, just as he had left it.

"Why, it's a kitten!" cried Jan's master, as he, too, reached the spot. "Poor little thing!"

He stooped down and picked up the tiny, limp body. "I think it's dead, Jan, but you did your best to save it. Didn't you?"

The dog watched intently, his tail waved slowly and his nose touched the hand that was gently rubbing the wet fur. Then, without any warning, the kitten's eyes opened and blinked and it uttered a faint mew.

"Well! I declare, it's alive after all!" the captain exclaimed. "It must have been washed ashore from some wrecked boat, judging from that driftwood raft. Looks most starved to death, Jan. If there's any truth that cats have nine lives, this little thing must have used up a good many of its lives getting to land. Come along, Jan! We'll try to save what's left, anyway."

The dog scampered toward the bungalow,

running back at times to leap about the old man. Jan was so happy that he had saved the poor little thing. It was only a little, grey kitten, and at the Hospice, of course, the dogs saved people; but that was in a place where there was snow.

When they all reached the kitchen, Jan crowded against the captain, who rubbed the shivering little cat with an old towel. Then it was placed on the floor with a saucer of milk. As the milk disappeared, the dog in his delight, moved closer, but the frightened animal humped up its back, fuzzed its thin tail and spit at him.

Of course, it did not know that Jan had saved its life, or that he did not want to hurt it, now. He moved away and sat down quietly to watch it. The saucer was filled with milk a second time, and the kitten's tongue lapped as fast as it could go. Its sides bulged out from its scrawny body when it had emptied the saucer and moved across the room.

"You poor little thing!" cried the old man, picking it up gently. "It's only got three legs, Jan!"

The poundmaster fixed his glasses and examined a hind leg which had no foot. "I guess it was born that way," he spoke. "Must have been taken on some boat as a mascot. Well, it doesn't matter what has happened to it, just so it's comfortable now, Jan!"

The kitten went back to the empty saucer, and sniffed at it, then with a funny little hop and jump, it came back and rubbed, purring, against the old man's leg, but it kept a sharp watch on the big dog.

"We'll call it Hippity-Hop," decided Captain Smith, and as neither the kitten nor Jan suggested a better name, that settled it.

Hippity-Hop was really quite a nice little kitten, even if she did not have as many legs as most cats have. Her fur was dark grey, a white breast and ring around her neck looked as though she had put on a clean shirt and collar, while every one of her three paws was snow-white, like nice white gloves. She spent a great deal of her time washing her fur with her tongue.

For many days Hippity-Hop was afraid of Jan, who was big enough to swallow her at one gulp; but when she learned that he stood back and let her eat first from his dish, although she had just cleaned her own plate, she lost her fear and grew to love him. Each night after supper she crawled between his paws and went to sleep, while he lay very still, that he might not waken his little friend.

Jan was very sure that Hippity-Hop was the nicest little kitten in the world, after she had learned one thing:

When first she went to live with the captain and Jan and had seen Cheepsie walking around on the floor, Hippity-Hop's green eyes glistened. Then her claws reached out from the fur that hid them and her tail twitched and jerked as she crouched to spring on the little yellow bird that was paying no attention to the kitten. But, just as she was ready to jump, there was a terrible roar behind her and she was grabbed by Jan's big jaws.

Hippity-Hop gave a yowl of fear, and twisted to scratch Jan's eyes, but he gripped her firmly, though his teeth did not hurt her. Captain Smith, hearing the commotion ran into the room and understood at once what had happened. He took the kitten from Jan, and though Hippity-Hop spit and scratched and yowled, the old man dipped her several times in a tub of water. Cats hate water, and Hippity-Hop hated water more than most cats, for it made her think of the time she had been almost drowned in the ocean.

"You've got to learn to be kind to Cheepsie, or else you can't live here with us," the old man said as he set the kitten on the porch floor.

The kitten began to lick her wet fur, but she was badly frightened and very sure that if Jan did not eat her up, the captain would put her back in the ocean again. So she resolved never to bother Cheepsie after that one time.

The bird seemed to understand, too, for it was not long after this that Hippity-Hop, Jan and Cheepsie ate out of the same dish. At times the bird would perch on the dog's head and sing to them all. Jan always sat as still as he could, until the song ended and Cheepsie had flown over to the captain's shoulder. Often the old man took his violin from the corner, and as he played he whistled or sang in a quavering voice, Jan's tail beat time on the floor, Hippity-Hop joined with a song of her own, though it was only a loud purr, while Cheepsie, perched on their loved master's shoulder, sang and trilled as loudly as he could, trying to make more music than the bird that lived in the violin.

"It's a fine old world, Jan!" the poundmaster would say, as he put the violin away in its box.

Then Hippity-Hop and Jan knew it was time for bed, and Cheepsie hurried to his cage and tucked his little head under his yellow wing.

Chapter VIII

THE MUZZLE

JAN'S curiosity about the dogs that disappeared was satisfied when a lady in a handsome gown was driven to the bungalow one evening.

Captain Smith met her with a happy smile, then he brought in an Airedale dog that had been with the other dogs for many weeks. The lady patted the dog, spoke to it gently, then she rose from her chair and the captain followed her to the gate where an automobile was waiting. The Airedale was lifted into the seat beside her.

"He will have the kindest care," she leaned forward to say, "and I hope you will be able to find homes for all the other dogs, too. I will tell my friends about them. Captain Smith, does the city pay for their feed while you find homes for them all?"

Jan saw his master slowly shake his head, "It does not take much to feed them," he answered.

"I am allowed to feed them a week, but I manage the rest of it from my salary. It makes me happy to see their gratitude, for most of them have been cuffed about so they don't know that there are people who will be kind and love them."

After the visitor left, Jan lay quietly watching the old man moving about the room. Now, he understood everything, and the dog rose quickly and thrust his nose into the wrinkled hand. The smile on the old man's face went deep into Jan's heart as the poundmaster, lifting the dog's head, looked into Jan's eyes, saying, "It's a pretty hard thing when any human being is without a friend, Jan; but people can speak up for themselves. A dog can't do that, and yet, he is the best friend any man can have."

So Jan always felt happy after that day, for when he missed one of the dogs now, he knew it had found a home and some one to love it. And on those days the poundmaster went around with shining eyes while his lips puckered up in a cheerful whistle, or Jan heard him singing:

"Old dog Tray is ever faithful,
    Grief cannot drive him away;
He's gentle and he's kind
And you'll never, never find
    A better friend than old dog Tray."

Many times when friends called to talk and smoke with the Captain, Jan would go for a short walk along the beach. One evening the ocean looked so inviting that the dog could not resist swimming far out, barking and snapping at floating kelp. It was much later than usual when he reached the shore and shook his long fur until it showered the salt water like a rain storm, then with a loud "Woof!" of happiness, he ran toward his home.

The high cliffs that rose above the beach threw dark shadows on the sand. The little bungalow where the captain lived was at the top of this cliff overlooking the ocean. The pound was not far away, and there were several other bungalows a little distance apart from each other, and a flight of wooden steps edged a twisting footpath which led directly up to the front gate of Jan's home.

It was easier to scamper up the pathway than climb the wooden steps, and the dog hurried to reach the top; but a slight noise made him pause and look at the thick brush near him. There was nothing to be seen, but Jan's ears listened sharply while his sensitive nose sniffed the air suspiciously. One sniff was enough to make the hair bristle along his back. William, his old enemy, was near.

Jan whirled quickly, his eyes shining with fury and hate, and his hair formed a stiff ridge along his back while his teeth gleamed in a snarl. Something slipped over his head and despite his struggles, it twisted tightly around his neck. A strange odor made him sick and weak when he tried to breathe. His paws clawed in his attempts to tear the sack from his head, so that he could breathe and fight, but his legs grew limp, a noise sounded inside his ears, something seemed to be hammering at the top of his head. He made one more effort, staggered a few steps, then crumpled down on the sand. But he knew it was William's boot that kicked him, and William's voice that said, "Guess that will settle you." Jan tried to growl but he was too sick to make a sound.

The next thing he knew was when he woke in a strange dark place. His whole body was stiff and sore, he felt sick all over and something hurt his nose terribly. His paws clawed at the thing that hurt. It was made of wire that cut deeply in his flesh. He knew it was a muzzle, for he had seen other dogs suffer from them. The more he clawed, the worse it hurt.

Then he rubbed his head sideways on the floor, but this made matters worse, so he gave up fighting and lay with his nose against the floor until he could stand the pain no longer. When he staggered to his feet, he found a rope held him, but when he tried to chew the rope the muzzle kept his jaws closed so that he was barely able to thrust the tip of his swollen tongue between his front teeth.

Jan suffered torture, not only because the wire cut his flesh, but also because any dog, when frightened, sick, or too hot, becomes feverish and his tongue hangs from his mouth. That is the way a dog sweats, and Prince Jan's mouth was clamped together by the muzzle. He could not hear any noise in the room, so he lay down and kept very quiet. There was really nothing else he could do, except howl. He knew that William had something to do with all this trouble, and he hated William more than ever.

A door opened. Jan sprang to his feet, hoping he might be able to break the rope and escape before the door was closed. He crouched and leaped with all his strength, but the rope was too strong and he fell with a thud to the floor, where he panted heavily. A flash of light almost blinded him, but he saw William and snarled defiance. Another man was in the room. Jan caught a glimpse of him, gave a sniff, and knew that this other man was the one who had been with William in the Pixley stable. He felt that he had two enemies now to fight.

As William came toward the dog, Jan strained on the rope.

"You'll get that temper taken out of you before long," threatened the man, at the same time keeping carefully beyond the length of the rope. But William's hatred outbalanced his caution, and he lifted his foot to give the dog a kick. Jan shrank back, not from fear as William supposed, but to get a better chance to spring and grab the man's leg.

"Let him alone," called the other man. "The worse you treat that dog the harder it will be to handle him."

William scowled. "The best thing is to kill him now. We're taking a big risk on the chance of selling him."

"Oh, go ahead and kill him if you want to," the other man shrugged his shoulders. "Let your spite keep you from making a thousand dollars."

He held out a bottle, "Here's the chloroform. Go on, finish the job if you're going to."

"I don't believe you can sell him," sneered William. "You just said that because you knew I was going to kill him before I left here."

"If you didn't hate dogs the way you do," replied Shorty, "you'd know that he'll sell for a thousand dollars as soon as he is over the Canadian line. The man I told you about will buy that dog without a question."

"Some one will recognize the dog before we get there, if the old man stirs things up."

"Not when I get him fixed," bragged Shorty.

"There's no time to fool with him," persisted William, "We've got to get away quick."

"Let me alone," snapped Shorty. "This is my end of the job. If you stop picking on the dog, I'll have no trouble with him. I never knew a dog from the time we were kids that didn't hate you on sight."

"Yes, and you're a regular fool over them," William retorted. "You take care of him and get the money for him, and I'll look out for the machine and sell that. But you've got to keep

that dog muzzled or there'll be trouble coming
your way fast and plenty. See?"

Shorty did not answer and William went out.
Jan and Shorty faced each other. The dog's
muscles were taut, his eyes alert. The man
looked at him steadily.

"You're the dandiest, spunkiest dog I ever
saw," he said at last, as though sure that Jan
understood the words. "I like you, old fellow,
and I'd turn you loose, if I dared."

He placed a pan of water in front of the dog
and the angry gleam softened in Jan's eyes. He
thrust his nose into the pan but the muzzle was
too tight to permit him to drink. The dog
looked up at Shorty, who reached out his hand.
Jan's tail waved, then he felt fingers run lightly
along his shoulders, fumble at the buckle of the
muzzle and the cruel thing fell to the floor. Before the dog lapped the water that he craved, he
stared into Shorty's face and saw a kindly smile
that told him this man was a friend. Jan's hot
tongue touched Shorty's hand before turning to
lap the cool liquid.

"You'll be all right now," Shorty said as he
rubbed the places where the strap had cut deeply.

Then when Jan had finished drinking, the man fed him bits of meat.

After the meal was over, Shorty took a pair of clippers and cropped Jan's long hair close to the skin. It did not hurt, so the dog submitted quietly. A sponge and bucket of dark liquid were brought by the man and Jan was thoroughly saturated, until the dye dripped to the floor.

"Got to put on that muzzle, boy, before he gets back," but this time the strips did not hurt so badly.

William chuckled when he saw the dog. "Great stunt, Shorty! The poundmaster wouldn't know his own dog if he caught him now!"

He picked up a couple of bundles and a suit-case, while Shorty led Jan by the rope. They were in a deep cañon, where no sound of the ocean could be heard. Jan did not know the place. He had never been away from the noise of the surf since living in California. A big, black automobile stood under a tree. William tossed the things into it and climbed to the front seat with a laugh.

"The police will have as much trouble finding a grey machine as the poundman will have finding a long-haired St. Bernard dog. We'll hit the road lively at night and camp in the day. There's just one thing you've got to remember. If I see you getting stuck on that dog I'm going to kill him. I'm taking him along because you said you could sell him, and I'm not going to stand any nonsense about it."

Shorty's only answer was to open the back door of the machine and motion the dog to jump. He obeyed and curled on the floor. Shorty sat in the back seat while William drove.

Jan did not sleep during the long, dark hours they sped over the road. He kept wondering what the captain would think, and hoping he could get back home some way. Once in a while he lifted his head as a flash of light showed another automobile passing. At daybreak William turned into thick brush and drove over rough ground until they stopped beside a shallow stream.

Still muzzled, Jan leaped from the car and followed Shorty, but he watched William closely. The dog was tied after he had been allowed to drink at the creek. William loafed while Shorty made coffee and cooked a meal, which the older man ate, grumbling all the time. Then he threw himself on the ground and dragged his hat over his face.

Shorty fed Jan, and after clearing away the breakfast things, moved closer to the dog. Jan's tail rustled the dry leaves and twigs, as Shorty, with a boyish smile, stretched on the ground beside him. A hand touched one of Jan's ears and pulled it gently, but the hand was friendly and the dog's eyes showed he understood. Then, tired from the long ride, Shorty and Jan slept soundly.

At dusk another meal was prepared and eaten, and they started again on their journey. For two more days and nights they travelled in the dark and camped in hidden places during the day, so that no one could see them. The muzzle was never taken again from Jan's nose, for William watched constantly and repeated his warnings several times. He did not know, however, that Shorty eased the strap so that the wire and leather could not cut, and in this way he made Jan as comfortable as was possible.

The night of the third day there was a full moon, and dim shadows were cast by scattered trees near the road. It was very warm and Jan's muzzle worried him; then, too, he was stiff from lack of the exercise to which he had been accustomed.   Shorty noticed the dog's restlessness and leaned down.   His fingers slipped under the strap and wires, then touched the buckle at the side of the head.   Jan squirmed nearer and wagged his tail.   Each night when they were well on the way, Shorty did this much to help the dog, but he had to tighten the muzzle before William turned the machine from the road to camp for the day.

As Shorty leaned over, the car reached a clear place in the road, where the moon shone brightly. Shorty did not see William turn, but a brutal fist struck full force against Shorty's face and he tumbled from the seat into the bottom of the automobile against Jan.

The dog growled, but the growl was meant for William, not Shorty.   Then Jan knew that Shorty was up on his feet and both men were swearing and fighting, while the automobile twisted from side to side of the road, and was going faster and faster.   There was a crash. Jan whirled over and over through the air and as he struck the ground he heard a man's scream of pain.   He did not know whether it was Shorty or William who cried out, but he did know that he was free, and he dashed into the darkness of the thick trees, not knowing where he was going, not caring where he went, only the one thing was in his mind—he was leaving William behind and he must run as fast as he could.

Chapter IX

AFTER the first wild dash for freedom, Jan settled to a steady jog for the rest of the night. When dawn came, some instinct made him turn into the brush where it grew most thickly. His one fear now was that William might find him. His one wish was to get back home. He did not know what kept him moving toward the south. He had nothing to guide him save the strange feeling that made him sure if he just kept on, some day he would reach the gate of the bungalow and see Hippity-Hop and the captain watching down the street for him.

Jan was able to lap water when he found it, but he could not fight, nor eat, even if he had found food, for the muzzle clamped his jaws together. He knew better now than to tug at it with his claws or rub it against the ground. The second night he was very hungry, but he started hopefully on his way, plodding steadily in the same direction. At dawn he was faint and weak from hunger and exhaustion, and when it grew dark again he did not want to move. Then he thought of the captain. Wearily Jan rose to his feet and with low-hanging head he dragged slowly along.

The fourth day after the escape, he was too weak to struggle further, and lay limp on the ground, with his eyes closed. He wanted to keep perfectly still, though he was suffering keenly from thirst, for he had not found any water that day. A rabbit darted from the thick brush close to Jan's head. The rustling of leaves made the dog's eyes open. He saw the little creature sit up in sudden fright, but Jan did not try to catch it, he was too tired and besides he knew that the muzzle held him a prisoner. So he watched the rabbit hop about him fearlessly, until the sound of steps in dry leaves startled it into the bushes.

Jan heard the steps, too. He thought William had found him, and knowing that he could not fight nor defend himself, he dragged himself wearily to his feet and staggered with trembling legs a few, short steps. Then he dropped heavily.

Voices sounded. Jan's ears lifted and quivered, his eyes brightened and his tail moved slightly. He was not afraid of children. They had always loved and petted him. Once more he rose and slowly pushed through the thicket to an open place where two little girls laughed and chattered as they picked wild blackberries into a small tin pail.

He edged toward the sunbonnets bobbing over the pail. The children heard the rustle and turned about, then the pail dropped, the berries spilled on the ground and the sunbonnet children ran, screaming wildly, "Father! Father! It's a big, black bear to eat all of us up!"

The dog halted, wondering why they ran from him. He heard a man's quick words, the children's excited voices and a woman's soothing tones.

"It's all right now!" thought poor Prince Jan. "Women and children won't hurt me."

He moved through the brush, but found himself looking straight into the barrel of a gun held by steady hands. Jan knew what that meant. His legs trembled as he pressed forward. Oh, if he could only make this man understand that he did not mean to hurt or frighten the little girls! He only wanted some one to take off this horrible muzzle.

The dog's pleading eyes were lifted to the man's face and then, unable to stand any longer, Jan fell weakly to the ground and pulled himself forward, inch by inch, to show that he meant no harm, and all the while his ragged tail kept beating very feebly. The man looked at him, then lowered the gun.

"Come here, girls! Your bear is only a lost dog!"

Jan did not look around at the patter of feet, but his paws went to the muzzle, and as he lay with his head against the man's feet, the pitifully pleading eyes and tugging paws of the dog spoke as plainly as words.

"Poor fellow!" said a gentle voice, then a woman's fingers worked carefully at the strap and Jan felt the muzzle fall away.

He touched her hand with his dry, stiff tongue, and saw the two little sunbonnet children, laughing, yet still afraid of the big dog, come to their mother's side. The man noticed the broken rope and examined the collar.

"No name or license," he spoke at last, "but somebody will be looking for him. I wonder how long he has been wandering around with this muzzle on him, poor chap!"

"Bring water, children," said the mother, "and the things that were left over from lunch. He must be hungry."

The tin pail was rescued from the ground and filled twice with water before Jan's thirst was slaked and he looked up with grateful eyes and dripping jaws. While he was drinking his fill, a basket had been opened by the children and slices of cold meat and bits of buttered bread were placed before him. He swallowed the food greedily, but paused between gulps to wag his tail and let them know how he thanked them.

For some time after this he lay quietly resting while the sunbonnet children sat close beside him and wondered where he came from and what his name was. Ruth, the younger, put out her hand to touch him timidly.

"I'm not afraid of him. He won't bite. He isn't a bear to eat us all up, is he, Charlotte?"

"I—— I—— aren't afraid, either," Charlotte's voice was uncertain, but her hand touched the dog's big head. Then both children lost all fear of him and Jan forgot about William and the hours of suffering, for the two little girls curled close to him, and soon they were all three fast asleep.

The sun was almost setting when the father and mother tucked the basket and shawls into the automobile. Jan watched with puzzled eyes as they carefully put away some little boards. He had noticed when he woke from his doze that both the man and the woman were sitting on stools with these boards propped before them, and they were making marks on them. The father was already in the machine and the little girls climbed in, then the mother put her foot on the step and Jan let out a wild howl that made them all start. He thought they were going to leave him behind and he knew that he could never run fast enough to follow them.

"Good gracious! What a howl!" exclaimed the man, laughing. "We won't leave you. Jump up, old chap!"

Jan lost no time scrambling into the automobile, then it ran swiftly along a smooth road which finally twisted through a beautiful cañon. Great trees were on all sides and a tiny stream bubbled and danced far below. Birds sang and rabbits dashed out of the brush with swift hops and jerks, but Jan did not want to eat the rabbits now. The children kept laughing and clapping their hands, calling to Jan, "Look, look, quick!" Sometimes their hands pressed his head to make him turn where they pointed.

Jan was very happy on that ride, but he still hoped that by and by he might get back home to Hippity-Hop and the captain.

Chapter X

The Home of the Sunbonnet Babies

THE home of Jan's new friends was perched high on the top of a mountain peak, far above the cañon through which they had driven. Jan heard them call this place Topango Pass. The house stood alone with overhanging oak trees and a garden full of flowers that made him think of the yard in front of the captain's bungalow.

A big stone fireplace was near the house, and pink geraniums grew closely around the little home, while over the porch climbed yellow roses that looked as if the fairies had hidden their gold among the green leaves.

"This is Roseneath," announced Charlotte to Jan as the automobile stopped in front of the porch and the two girls jumped out, followed by the dog.

"Charlotte!" Ruth said suddenly, stopping halfway up the path, "we've got to find a name for that dog right away!"

It was a very serious matter, so the children sat on the lowest step of the porch and Jan squatted before them. He wished he could help by telling his name and about the Hospice, but all he could do was to sit still and look from one eager little face to the other. After trying several names they decided on "Bruin."

"Because he is so big and black, just like a bear!"

Jan rather liked the name. It sounded like Bruno, but of course, the sunbonnet children did not know anything about Bruno and the Hospice, so they said Jan was very smart to remember the new name without any trouble at all.

The next morning he was wakened early by the children's voices and hurried to meet them in front of the house. Charlotte had a tin bucket in her hand and Jan wondered if they were going to pick more berries. But they went down a path that led to the stable and then he stood still in surprise.

Right in front of them was a strange creature about the size of a common dog. It had long, white hair, a white beard like a very old man's, two horns curved back over its head and its feet had sharp-pointed hoofs. It was tied by a rope and back of it was a smaller animal of the same kind.

Charlotte went past the larger one and sat down on a little wooden stool beside the smaller animal and soon the tin pail was full of milk. Back to the house trotted the children, and Jan, very much puzzled, kept beside them. In the kitchen they found the mother cooking breakfast. Jan lifted his nose and sniffed at the odor of broiling steak and hot biscuit.

"Milk for the berries we picked yesterday," the mother of the sunbonnet children said smiling. "Won't we have a fine breakfast this morning! And there's a nice bone in the steak for Bruin, too!"

She poured a little milk into a pan and placed it on the floor for Jan. He knew that the white animal must have been a cow, yet it was not like the cow at the Pixleys' home, but when he tasted the milk, it was just as nice as the big, yellow cow's milk.

While breakfast was being eaten, the children and their parents chatted together and Jan looked about the place. The walls of the rooms were hung with beautiful pictures, among them many fat little babies with sunbonnets hiding their faces. He was sure that if the sunbonnets were pushed back he would see the faces of Ruth and Charlotte laughing at him.

As time went by Jan was quite happy and learned to love his gentle playmates very dearly. He grew accustomed to seeing the artists sitting before boards, painting pictures like those on the walls. Even the little girls, Ruth and Charlotte, sometimes sat on the ground and made him lie still while they worked away with pencils and pieces of paper and told him they were making his picture to put in a book. It did not quite explain matters to Jan when Ruth held up one of these papers in front of his nose and said, "You see, Bruin, we're going to be ill——us——trators like mother when we grow up, and then we'll put you in a book, maybe!"

After Jan had several good baths the ugly black dye began to wear off and his white shirt-front and paws and the white streak on his nose showed plainly. Then the rusty black fur on his entire body became its natural tawny red and grew rapidly. The Melvilles now realized that Jan had been stolen and often wondered who had lost him. They asked the few people they saw but none of them had heard of such a dog, so the family felt that Jan belonged to them.

Ruth and Charlotte were much interested when their parents told them that Bruin was a St. Bernard dog, and all about the noble animals that lived at the Hospice, for the two artists had visited the place many years before Ruth or Charlotte had been born. When their mother finished telling them these things, Ruth exclaimed, "Mother! Then you and daddy and Charlotte and me are all St. Bernard dogs, because we found Bruin when he was lost, didn't we?"

Jan was not the only pet of this family. The "Melville Menagerie" was what their mother called the collection of animals. There were two grown-up goats, named Captain Kidd and Mrs. Cream; two baby-goats, Peaches and Strawberry; a mother cat named Chicago, because she was smoke color, and her three kittens, Texas, California, and Pennsylvania. Next was the canary bird, Pitty-Sing, and last, but not least, five horn-toads which were nameless, but who lived peacefully together in a box with sand to burrow in.

All of these members of the family interested

Jan, but he wanted to be friends with the old cat and her kittens, because he missed Hippity-Hop. Whenever he tried to go near them, the four jumped to their feet, arched their backs, and spat at him so rudely that he gave up making friends, and decided that only three-legged cats liked dogs.

Each day about three o'clock all work was put aside by the artists, for this was the time they went to visit "The Land of Make-Believe." Sometimes they were gypsies, and supper was cooked over a campfire among the oak trees. Again, they pretended Jan was a big bear and he found it great fun to chase after the children while they ran away as though really afraid of him. Then it was "Little Red Riding Hood" with Jan for the wolf, but he did not eat any one, like the wolf did, for he knew he would have a nice piece of meat cooked over the wood fire as they all sat about on the ground and pretended they had no place to sleep excepting underneath the trees. When the stars began to twinkle, the sunbonnet children said that the angels were lighting the candles in Heaven, and very soon it was time to go home for the night.

Haying time in California is different from

that of other parts of the world, for it is in May, and many months ahead of other places. The fields were dotted with little mounds of yellow hay drying in the sun, and one evening Mrs. Melville told the children she had a new game for the Land of Make-Believe. The next afternoon they could hardly wait until they reached the hay-fields.

"Now, children," said their mother, "these are the snow-covered peaks of the Alps that I told you about. Ruth must be a lost traveller and wander around among these mountains of snow until she is too tired to go any further. Then she must lie down and pull the hay over her and wait to be rescued from death in the snow."

As Ruth scampered away, Jan followed her, but Mrs. Melville called him back. He sat looking at her, but his head turned frequently toward the place he had last seen little Ruth. Several times he started to get up, but each time he sat down again and waited.

"You, Charlotte, are a monk from the Hospice and Bruin will go with you to search for lost travellers in this terrible snow-storm."

Jan stood very still, but his tail flapped around in circles while Mrs. Melville fastened a canteen of water to his collar, then she said, "Now, Bruin, go find Ruth!"

"Woof! Woof!" rang out the big voice, just as the dogs of the Hospice called when they started on the trail. Followed closely by Charlotte, Jan led the way from one hay mound to another, poking his nose deeply into each. Charlotte kept calling, "Find Ruth, Bruin! Go find her! She's lost in the snow and will freeze to death if we don't find her soon!"

Jan forgot it was only the Land of Make-Believe, while he burrowed into the haycocks. As he ran from one to the other, his bark sounded again and again, for he remembered the lessons Brother Antoine had given him and Rollo, and the canteen that bumped against his breast felt like the little wooden casket he had carried on the trail. At last he found the lost traveller. Jan lifted his head and uttered a sharp bark of triumph before his nose began tossing the hay that completely covered Ruth.

"He found her! He found her!" shrieked Charlotte in greatest excitement, just as though Ruth had really been lost in the snow-drifts.

Both parents ran to watch the game and Ruth's face appeared in the hay, like a pink

Easter egg in a nest. She squinted up, saw her mother and father, Charlotte and Jan, then remembered that she was lost and shut her eyes quickly. Jan touched her cheek with his nose, and licked her face. She could not keep still any longer, because she wanted to sneeze and that would spoil the whole game. So she opened her eyes, put up her hand and unfastened the canteen from Jan's collar and swallowed such a big gulp of water that she almost choked. Her arms went about Jan's neck and while she clung, he moved slowly away from the mound, his tail waving rapidly and his big eyes full of pride. Ruth had been saved from a terrible death in the snowdrifts of the Alps!

The whole party of rescuers hastened to the Hospice under the trees, where supper was almost ready, and as they sat around the outdoor fireplace waiting the meal, they all declared that Bruin had acted just as if he had really lived at the Hospice and knew all about the dogs there and how they worked.

Three months after Jan went to live at Roseneath, the family sat reading one evening, and Jan sprawled at their feet. Ruth and Charlotte were deeply interested in the pictures of a new magazine for children, and Mr. Melville held a newspaper. He had been to the nearest town that day and had brought the mail home with him.

Suddenly he let the paper drop to his lap and sat looking at Prince Jan, then he picked up the paper again, saying, "Listen to this!"

All of them turned expectantly, for the parents always read aloud anything that might interest the children.

CAPTURED THIEF WORRIES OVER LOST DOG

John Leavitt, alias Shorty, now held as one of the two men who stole and wrecked an automobile belonging to Paul R. Wallace of Los Angeles, has made a confession implicating his half-brother, William Leavitt, formerly stableman at the beach-home of the Pixleys.

According to Shorty's statement, they had stolen a St. Bernard dog from Captain Smith, the Poundmaster, intending to sell the animal in Canada. Shorty became attached to the dog, Prince Jan, and in a quarrel with his brother over the muzzling of the dog, the machine was wrecked.

Leavitt evidently supposed Shorty was dead beneath the wreckage, and escaped. Shorty was found later, seriously injured, and his recovery was not expected. His one anxiety seems to be that Prince Jan, being muzzled, might have died of starvation. Any one knowing the fate of the dog is asked to communicate with Captain Smith, through this paper.

Prince Jan is a pure St. Bernard, with long fur, but he had been clipped and his hair dyed black.

No trace of William Leavitt has been found, but the

authorities are looking for him. He has a criminal record in the East and is now wanted there. Shorty has been bound over for trial.

The family looked at the dog sleeping peacefully at their feet.

"Not the least doubt," said Mr. Melville.

"Call him, Ruth. Call his name—Prince Jan —and see how he acts."

The child's lips quivered and her eyes filled with tears as she went to her mother's side. "But, mother, if he is Prince Jan, will somebody take him away from us?"

Charlotte's eyes, too, were blurred and her lower lip dropped.

"Suppose," the mother spoke gently, and her arm went about the slender little figure leaning against her in half-choked grief, "Suppose, dear, some one found you when you were lost, and daddy and I didn't know where you were, and the people couldn't understand when you tried to tell them who you were and where we lived," the voice grew very tender and grave, "and then the people found out where you belonged and that we were looking everywhere for you, and grieving because we did not know whether you were hungry and unhappy. Do you think it would be right for them to keep you away from us, even if they did love you very, very dearly?"

Ruth's head hung low and nobody spoke until she lifted her face with a tear-wet smile, "Jan! Prince Jan!" she called in her high, sweet voice.

They saw the muscles of the sleeping dog twitch. The big paws moved slightly, as though in his dreams he was running to answer that name. His tail threshed lightly on the floor, but still he slept.

"Jan, Prince Jan!" both children now called.

He leaped to his feet. Quivering with excitement he faced them.

"Jan!" repeated Mr. Melville.

The dog darted to the man's side and stood with eager, expectant eyes and furiously switching tail. When he heard the name from Mrs. Melville, Jan ran to her and laid his head on her knee, looking into her face questioning her dumbly.

"He knows his name! He is Prince Jan!" the children cried as they swooped down on him with squeezes and hugs, while the dog whined and twisted and uttered sharp barks of excitement until they were all laughing at him.

"Do you want to go home to the captain,

Jan?" Mrs. Melville leaned over him as she spoke.

"Woof! Woof!" he answered promptly, and they all knew that he meant "Yes."

So Mr. Melville got pen and ink and wrote to the poundmaster, telling that Prince Jan was safe and well, and that he, himself, would bring the dog home.

That was how Prince Jan came back to the captain and Hippity-Hop, at last. He was very happy at going home, yet he looked back wistfully at Ruth and Charlotte standing on the porch waving their hands, as the automobile drove away from the Land of Make-Believe, where Jan had been so kindly treated. But when he saw the ocean again and the road up the bluff and knew that he was near the bungalow, he was ready to leap from the machine and dash madly to the place where the captain, Hippity-Hop, and Cheepsie lived. He knew then that he loved them more than anybody in the whole world.

Chapter XI

Prince Jan Visits Shorty

JAN reached the front gate and let out a ringing "Woof" of joy that brought the captain and Hippity-Hop out at once. The old man's arms went about Jan's neck, and the dog gave little whines of delight, his tongue touched the wrinkled hands, and his tail went around so fast that it did not look like a tail, but just a blur of fuzzy hair.

When Mr. Melville was seated, and the Captain on a chair near by, Jan's head rested on the old man's knee and the toil-worn fingers stroked the dog's soft fur. Hippity-Hop rubbed against Jan's legs, purring like a noisy little buzz-saw, and Cheepsie flew down from his cage to perch first on the shoulder of the captain and then on Prince Jan's head, while a flood of bird-music filled the little room.

"I wish the children could see Jan now!" said Mr. Melville, and then he told the captain about

114

"I wish the children could see Jan now!"

finding Jan and the story in the paper that had brought the dog back to his master.

Hippity-Hop had been very lonely after Jan's disappearance, and the dog did not dream that the three-legged kitten had mewed and mewed for him until the old captain picked her up in his arms and said, "He will come back to us some day, Hippity-Hop." And each day the old man, with the kitten at his side, sat on the front porch watching down the road.

The morning after Jan's return, Mr. Melville came again to the bungalow and he and the captain called Jan to get in the automobile with them. Hippity-Hop's forlorn little face peered between the curtains of the front window, but none of them heard her plaintive cry as they all vanished from her sight. When the automobile stopped, Jan saw a grey building of stones with windows crossed by iron bars. He followed his friends into a large room where several men were seated. They spoke to the captain and Mr. Melville, and all looked at Jan, patting his head for some reason, as they talked of him.

Then Jan, the captain, and Mr. Melville followed another man through long dim hallways that had doors on either side, very close together.

One of these doors was unlocked, and as Jan and his friends passed through, the door was shut and locked again.

They were in a dingy room with grey walls, the only window being high up and criss-crossed by bars. It was a very small window. On a cot in a corner of the room sat a man. He turned his head toward them and when he saw the dog, he jumped to his feet, calling, "Jan!"

"Woof!" answered the dog in surprise as he leaped toward the man.

Shorty dropped on his knees and took Jan's head between his hands, talking to the big dog as though talking to a little child whom he loved very dearly. Jan did not know, nor would he have cared had he known, that Shorty was in jail. He only knew that this was his friend who had tried to protect him from William's abuse. And all the while, Captain Smith and the artist were watching them with kindly eyes.

At last, Shorty rose and sat on his narrow cot, with his two visitors on either side, and Jan, planted right in front of Shorty, turned his head from one to the other as though he were trying to understand what they were talking about so earnestly. Shorty's hand stroked Jan's head, and every once in awhile the man would say, "I'm so glad you found him."

"You love dogs, don't you?" asked the old poundmaster, as they rose to go.

Shorty looked down at Jan for a second, then answered, "I never had any friends in my life excepting dogs."

They left Shorty alone in the little grey room and went back to the men in the big room, where the sun streamed across the floor like a tiny river of gold, but back in the other room the window was so high and so small that the sun could not shine through it at all. Shorty did not think about that now.

The captain talked to the men, who listened attentively, and finally he said, "Judge, I don't believe that any one who loves dogs and is kind to them is bad all the way through. Shorty says he never had a friend in his life except dogs."

"I do not think he is naturally bad," answered the judge, who sat in a big chair back of a high desk. "From what I can learn, he has been under William Leavitt's control since they were children. Shorty tried to get away from his brother twice, but each time William found and punished him so brutally that the boy was afraid to venture again. There are scars on Shorty's feet made by a hot iron the last time he tried to escape from his brother. Shorty is not quite nineteen yet. That is how he comes under the Juvenile Court."

"Judge," exclaimed the captain, his face alight with eager pleading, "you know there's lots of people that folks call bad, who would be decent if they had a chance. Can't you give Shorty a chance to show that he wants to make good? Send him some place where his brother can't find him?"

"Your Honor," the artist spoke now, "if there is any way to arrange it, I would like to take the lad up to Roseneath and we will try to help him make good in our Land of Make-Believe, as we call our home."

Jan did not understand what they were saying, but he knew it had something to do with Shorty and that the captain was talking very earnestly, so the dog edged between his two friends and stood watching the man at the high desk, for all in the room were looking at him. This man was very quiet, and seemed to be thinking, then he looked up and said, "Bring Shorty in here."

A few minutes passed in silence, then the door swung open and Shorty shuffled through it. He blinked in the bright sunlight and ducked his head as though he were afraid to look up at them all. Jan moved quickly and pushed his nose into Shorty's hand. The face above him lighted with a sudden, winning smile. The judge watched them both but did not speak. Then Shorty remembered where he was and raised his head to face the man on the high platform. That man was looking with very kindly eyes at the lad and the dog.

"Shorty," the judge spoke very plainly, "if I give you two years' suspended sentence and let you go with Mr. Melville to live on his ranch, will you try to make good?"

Shorty only stared stupidly. The judge repeated his words more slowly and added, "We will not let it be known where you are, so you need have no fear of William. I want to know if you will give me your solemn promise—your word of honor—to do your very best?"

Shorty's face twitched, his eyes blinked fast, his hands reached out as if he were feeling for some other hand to grasp. The hands hesitated, groped, then one hand moved upward across his face as though to brush something away that kept him from seeing plainly. Those in the room watched but made no sound.

"Do you mean it, Judge?" the lad's voice was low and husky, but there was a tone of pleading in it. "You ain't just fooling, are you, Judge?"

"No," the judge spoke very firmly, "I'm not fooling, Shorty. You are going to get your chance."

They saw Shorty fling himself down on his knees beside Prince Jan and pull the dog close to him, while racking sobs shook the boy's shoulders. Jan twisted around to lick Shorty's face and comfort him, for the dog did not know his friend was crying from happiness. At last Shorty rose to his feet, brushing away the tears with his ragged coat sleeve.

"Judge, I promise you I'll make good or I'll die in the trying," he said, and all those who heard him knew he would do his best.

The judge stepped down from the big chair and put his hand on the boy's shoulder, saying in a kindly voice, "You're bound to make good, Shorty, and we are all your friends!"

The other men shook Shorty's hand, and the judge said, with a smile, "I have a nice collie

pup up at my home that I will give you, if **Mr.
Melville** doesn't object."

"We have no dog, now that Prince Jan is
gone," the artist answered quickly, "and I promised my wife that I would bring back some kind
of a dog for the children. They would be lonesome now, without one. So the pup will be just
as welcome as Shorty will be."

Shorty forgot this man was a judge, and
smiled at him, asking, "What's the pup's name,
please?"

"He is a registered pup with a long fancy
name, but we just call him 'Pup,' so you can pick
out a name to suit yourself."

"I'm going to call him 'Prince Jan'!" announced the boy, and all agreed that it was a fine
name for any pup.

They shook hands once more with Shorty and
wished him good luck, and when the boy walked
from the room, he held his head high. A smile
was on his lips and hope in his eyes. Mr. Melville walked beside him.

That evening when Jan, Hippity-Hop,
Cheepsie, and the captain were sitting together,
the old man looked at the dog and said, "Jan,
your ancestors rescued travellers from the snow,

but to-day you helped Shorty get a new start in life, and that is a bigger thing than if you had saved him from death in the Alps."

The dog did not understand the words, but he knew that the smile was the same happy smile that came when the old poundmaster had found a good home for one of the friendless dogs. So Jan was happy, too.

Chapter XII

The Poundmaster's Problem

FOR several days after Shorty had gone on his way to the Land of Make-Believe with Mr. Melville, life ran very quietly and happily for Prince Jan and his friends in the little bungalow on the cliffs. Then he began to notice that Captain Smith was worried, and when Jan poked his nose into the hand of his friend, though the hand stroked the dog's head, the poundmaster did not smile and his eyes looked as if he saw something Jan could not see. It worried Jan, though he could do nothing but lie quietly with his anxious eyes fixed on the old man's face.

One evening after supper a loud knock at the door caused the dog to look up quickly, while Hippity-Hop jumped with fuzzed tail and excited eyes. The captain opened the door and two men came in. They shook hands with him and sat down in the chairs he pushed forward. The two men looked around the room, stared at the dog, then turned to Jan's master. The look on the poundmaster's face made the dog feel certain that these men had something to do with the old man's worry, so Jan went over and sat close to him, resting his big head on the captain's knee.

"Is that the dog that was stolen?" one of the visitors asked at last.

"Yes," replied the captain. "This is Prince Jan. He was sent to the pound almost dead with mange and orders through the stableman that the dog was to be killed because he was vicious. But," the poundmaster smiled down at the dog that was gazing with loving eyes into his face, "you see, all he needed was kind treatment and proper care."

"I understand, Smith," the other man now spoke in a voice that sounded cross to Jan, "that you are violating the City ordinances, and are keeping the dogs that are brought to the pound. They are sent here to be killed, not kept."

"I find homes for them all," the old man hastened to say, "and it only takes a short time to find people who will give them good homes. Not one of the dogs that has been brought here since I had charge has been vicious. Those that seemed dangerous at first grew gentle and kind as soon as they found no one would hurt them."

"Of course, we know how you feel about them, but the City hires you to kill the dogs if their owners do not claim or want them. People complain that you keep the dogs and feed them at the public expense. We can't have that, you know."

Captain Smith rose, and the hand he held out suddenly toward the two men was trembling. "I don't know who told you that," he said earnestly, "and I don't believe that whoever did say it meant to tell an untruth, but the only dogs that are fed at public cost are those for which I am allowed money. After any dog has been with me for more than a week, I pay for his food myself."

The two strange men looked at each other and were silent a few minutes. Finally one of them spoke again.

"I'm sorry, Smith, but you will have to get rid of the dogs. The pound is not a boarding place for stray dogs, and the fact that you pay for their feed after a certain time does not change matters."

The old man sat down in his chair as though he were very tired, and stared at the floor until he felt Jan's nose, and then he looked into the dog's sympathetic eyes. The wrinkled hand twitched, but the old man's kindly face turned to the other man.

"I know you can't change the law," he said slowly, "but if you could let me have a little more time, I can find homes for all the dogs that are here now. There are only ten, beside Prince Jan, and he belongs to me. See"—he pushed aside the thick hair on the dog's neck—"I bought a collar and a license for him, and he has never eaten a mouthful of food except what I have paid for myself."

"Too many people have complained," was the reply. "The dogs are noisy, and no one is allowed to have so many dogs inside the city limits. You know it is against the law, Smith. That settles it."

Both men rose to their feet and looked at the old man, but at the door they stopped and talked together in low voices. Then one of them turned and said, "We don't want to be too hard on you, for we know you love dogs, so we will give you two days to find places for them. After that, the dogs that are still here must be killed, or you will have to resign your position as poundmaster."

Smith watched them go down the pathway to the front gate, then with low drooping head and slow steps he went back to the little room. Jan pressed closely against him as the old man sank into his chair. Cheepsie flew from his cage and perched on the captain's shoulder, singing loudly, and Hippity-Hop, not to be left from the little family group, limped across the room and rubbed, purring, against the old pound-master's leg. They knew that he was troubled, and all of them tried to make him understand they were sorry for him and loved him.

"We've got to do something for those poor dogs," he said to Jan, at last. "Even if I do give up my job it won't help them, now. I can't find homes for them all in such a short time, Jan. Nearly every one I know here has a dog already, and some of them have two. Folks have been mighty good taking my dogs."

Cheepsie sang an answer, Hippity-Hop purred her reply, and Prince Jan's tail, thumping the floor, said very plainly that he agreed with his master. The captain smiled at them all, for he understood their languages. "It's bound to work out right, somehow," he asserted cheerfully, and again his three dumb friends answered him.

The next morning Captain Smith left Jan and Hippity-Hop in the front yard. It was the first time the old man had ever carried his violin with him, and he trudged briskly down the street, only stopping when he reached a corner to wave his hand back where Jan and the kitten stood with noses pushed between the pickets of the fence. Jan was worried because it was the first time the captain had gone away from the house without him.

So, while Hippity-Hop climbed trees, chased butterflies, and washed her face and paws many times, the dog kept perfectly quiet, watching for his master's return. A big bark welcomed the captain home as Jan ran down the street to meet him.

"Come along, Jan," the old man was smiling, and the dog trotted beside him into the pound, where the other dogs pulled on their ropes and greeted them noisily.

The poundmaster stopped in front of each dog and fastened a small metal tag to its collar, then he took them all into his own back yard, where they crowded and leaped about him or chased each other in play. One dog was so happy that he kept turning around and around after his own short tail until he was too dizzy to stand up.

"It's a pretty good-sized family, Jan," laughed the old man, as he sat in a chair on the back porch, smoking his pipe and watching the dogs' antics. "They've all got licenses now, so no one can order any of 'em killed for a year. I guess we can find homes for all of them before that time is up."

So, when the two men came again, Captain Smith took them into the back yard and showed the license on each dog's collar, as he said, "I have found homes for five of them already, and to-morrow I'll take the others to a friend in the country. He will look out for them until we have good places for all."

He smiled happily at the dogs, then looked up at the two men, but his smile faded at their next words.

"Well, what do you intend doing with the next bunch you collect?"

"Why, I'll get homes for them, like these others."

"That won't do, Smith. Either you've got to take care of the work as you are ordered, or else let some other man have your place. What are you going to do about it?"

Smith's hand rumpled the fur on Jan's back. The eyes of the dog and the old man met, then the poundmaster lifted his head and said quietly, "I will give up the place. I thought when I took this work that it would give me a chance to make some poor dumb brutes a little happier and more comfortable, but I never intended to shoot one of them. Why, I couldn't do that. They're all my friends!"

"All right," was the answer. "Suit yourself. We'll have another man take charge to-morrow morning."

Without further words the men left, and the captain, followed by Jan, went into the back yard where the ten dogs rushed to meet them. Barking, leaping, tumbling over each other, they struggled to get close to the old man who stood smiling and patting them, while he said softly, "The best friends a man ever had, Jan."

Prince Jan looked at the bunch of dogs, little dogs, big dogs, curs, and dogs of high breeding. No matter where they had come from, they had

found a protector in the old poundmaster, but
they did not know that he had given up his position because he would not kill them. Even Jan
did not know what his master was writing that
evening. It took some time to get the letter just
right, then it was folded, placed in an envelope,
sealed and stamped, and Jan walked with the
captain to the letter-box several blocks away.

When they were home again, the old man sat
smoking his pipe and nodding, then he got up
and wound the clock, for it was Saturday night.
As he put the key on top of the clock, he said,
"Well, Jan, we'll have to hunt for another job
on Monday, but I don't think it will take long
for us to find something we can do."

Monday morning people came for the dogs,
and the captain patted each of his four-footed
friends, before it went to its new home. A man
from a ranch brought an automobile, and into
this the five dogs which had not yet found per-
manent homes were lifted. Then the captain
took out his worn pocketbook and counted
money, which he handed to the rancher.

"Take good care of them for me," said the old
man, "and I'll pay for their food until we find
homes for them all."

"All right, Smith," the man answered, and then he drove away with the yelping dogs.

It was very quiet in the house and back yard, but Hippity-Hop was glad of it. She had not enjoyed herself while there were so many dogs in the back of the house. After lunch was over, the captain dressed himself in his best clothes, put on his hat, and with Jan at his side, went to many big buildings where he talked earnestly with several men.

They were very kind to him, patted Jan, and promised they would let the captain know if they saw any work he could do. Jan saw that his old friend seemed tired after they had been to several places, and when the dog thrust his nose into the captain's hand, the faded eyes would smile bravely, as the captain said, "It's bound to work out right in the end, Jan."

Day after day, they made these trips, and at night Jan lay watching the face of his master, but the smile was not seen very often now. One evening the old man was more despondent than ever, so even Jan's wistful sympathy failed to rouse him, though the hand caressed the dog. Jan's heart ached, and unable to stand it longer,

he pushed his head on the captain's knee and
gave a low whimper.

Captain Smith leaned down and lifted the
dog's head between his hands and looking into
his puzzled eyes, he said slowly, "We're up
against it, Jan. My money is gone, and there
does not seem to be any work for me to do.
Every one is very kind, and all promise to send
for me, but it is just because they are sorry. If
I were younger, it would be easy to find plenty
to do."

Jan licked the gnarled hand and tried to show
that he wished he could help, but the only thing
he could do was to show the love and sympathy
that filled his loyal heart. That night when the
light was out and everything was quiet, Jan lay
wide awake trying to puzzle out what it all
meant, and then he heard a faint sigh and knew
that the captain, on his cot, was awake, too. So
the dog rose softly and moved to the side of the
narrow bed, where he stretched himself on the
floor. Presently he felt a hand touch his head
and he turned quickly to caress it with his
tongue. Then he heard the old man say, "It's
bound to work out right some way, Jan!"

The next morning the captain was more

cheerful, and when the postman came along the street, the old man called out, "It's a beautiful day, isn't it?"

The postman nodded, then said, "I have a registered letter for you, Captain."

With surprised eyes and quick steps, the old man reached the gate and signed the card. He turned the letter over, stared at it, then smiled and cried out, "It's from my daughter!"

A happy smile illumined his face and his fingers were unsteady as he tore open the envelope, saying, "She and her husband went to Alaska two years ago. I haven't heard anything from them for six months. You see, when winter begins up there, the river freezes solid, so no boats or mail can reach them."

"Well, the postmen up there have an easy time once in a while," replied the letter-carrier as he slung the heavy pouch over his shoulder and went on his way.

The old man sat on the step of the porch and read the letter, which was a long one. Jan knew his master was glad over something, and yet, when the letter was finished, there were tears rolling down the captain's cheeks. Jan edged tightly against him.

"They're all well," said the old man, "and they want us to come and live with them. Look, Jan!" He held out a piece of paper which the dog sniffed at. "That is to pay our way, and we're going to start just as soon as we can pack up. You see, it worked out right in the end!"

Busy hours followed for them all. The captain hurried about the little house, packing things into boxes, and taking down pictures, which he put into a trunk. One picture he held for some minutes, "That was Jenny when she was a little girl, just able to walk, Jan." Then he wrapped it very carefully in a faded blue knitted scarf and placed it in the trunk with the other things. Hippity-Hop scurried about the room, and Cheepsie had a hard time clinging to the old man's shoulder, for he moved so swiftly and kept leaning over the trunk.

It was three o'clock in the afternoon when the trunk was shut and locked and an old carpet-bag stood beside it. The captain's hat was on his head, Cheepsie chirped in his cage that was wrapped tightly with paper, and Hippity-Hop mewed forlornly from a basket, while Jan moved nervously between the bundles and his master, wondering what it all meant. Then a man drove to the door and carried the trunk and valise to his wagon, leaving the captain to pick up the bird-cage and the hamper that held the kitten.

"Come along, Jan," he called cheerfully, and the dog rushed ahead, turning back to frisk in circles or leap up in front of his friends. Jan was much happier than Hippity-Hop, who was yowling loudly as she stuck one paw through a hole in the basket, and Cheepsie's twitters sounded really cross.

Jan, once again, was put in a baggage car and after a ride of several hours, the captain got him out and led him to a wharf. Jan remembered his trip in the boat when he came to the Land of No Snow. He hesitated to go up the plank walk, but the captain smiled and said, "It's all right, Jan. Come along!" and then the dog trotted fearlessly along the boards that led to the deck of the big boat. Everything was confusion, but Jan did not worry when his master led him down into the lower part of the boat, under the deck. After tying Jan, the old man gave him a final pat and said, "I'll be back soon, Jan"; and the dog, knowing everything was all right, stretched on his side and closed his eyes.

He was tired from the trip, the excitement of packing, and from those days of worry before the letter came that made the captain happy again. So he was very glad to have nothing to do, nothing to think about.

Then the boat trembled and puffed, and Prince Jan knew that he and Hippity-Hop and Cheepsie and their loved master were going somewhere together, and he was satisfied.

Chapter XIII

THE VOICES OF THE HOSPICE DOGS

PRINCE JAN could not tell how many days and nights passed while the boat throbbed on its way. He grew accustomed to the motion and as the captain came often each day to see him and talk to him, and many other people also visited him, Jan found life very pleasant.

Among his visitors was a pretty young woman with big brown eyes and a gentle voice. Nearly always a little child was in her arms, or held by the hand, for it was just beginning to walk. Captain Smith and these two seemed to be great friends. Many times he carried the baby in his arms and it laughed up in his face when he held it down to pat Jan's head. The dog watched for them every day, and he was never disappointed. Once, the captain brought Hippity-Hop to see Jan, and the kitten purred loudly and rubbed against the dog's legs, while Jan poked her gently with his nose. The old man chuckled, "You haven't forgotten each other, have you?" Then he picked up the kitten and carried it away.

That night, without warning, everything seemed to change, somehow. The boat leaped and jumped as though it were frightened at the big waves that washed against and over it. The night was dark, and down in the hold of the vessel it was still darker. Jan listened to men running overhead, voices called loudly and then came a sudden crash. The boat quivered as though it were hurt.

Jan was thrown so heavily against the side of the boat that he lay gasping for breath, then he dragged himself to his feet. Swaying with the jerky motion, but managing to brace himself, he peered through the inky darkness toward the steps leading to the deck. Again he heard the hurried feet, the loud voices of men, and this time there were cries of women and children, too.

He knew something was not right, and as he pulled with all his strength on the rope that held him, and strained his eyes toward the stairway, he heard a sound that made him give a loud bark of joy.

"All right, Jan!" his master was calling through the darkness, "I'm coming!"

The dog whimpered and licked the hands that fumbled at the rope which was tied to the side of the boat. With a leap and yelp of joy, Jan scrambled up the stairs ahead of his master, and both of them reached the deck.

It was very early in the morning and the sky was heavy with dark clouds. The wind screamed and big waves tossed so high that at times the boat appeared to be down in the bottom of a great hole. Although the vessel jerked, groaned, creaked and crunched, it did not move forward. When the water washed back a few minutes, Jan saw jagged rocks poking up and felt the boat pounding on them. He could not understand it at all, and as he looked up with puzzled eyes at his master, he saw the old man was staring straight ahead at a strip of land not very far away, where a lot of people were running about in a great hurry.

One of the boat crew ran past Jan, carrying a rope. Other men were fastening queer looking rings about the bodies of women and children, while still more men were lowering a little boat into the water. But as soon as it touched the waves, it was turned on end and smashed like an egg-shell against the side of the ship. Jan, standing with his legs braced firmly, saw the frightened women and children huddled together. Most of them were very quiet, but some were crying. A few were kneeling on the wet deck, and though their eyes were shut, Jan knew they were not asleep, for their lips were moving as if they were talking to some one whom he could not see.

The shore did not seem very far away, and Jan saw men pushing a little boat into the water. They leaped into it quickly and grabbed up oars.

"Thank God!" said the old poundmaster to a man who stood beside him and Jan. "The Life Guards will save the women and children!"

"There is no Life Saving Station here," Jan heard a woman's voice reply. He looked up and saw the pretty lady beside his old master. Her face was very white and she held her baby tightly in her arms, while she stared at the place where the tiny boat was being shoved into the sea by men who stood waist-deep in the rushing water. Then the boat shot high on a wave and started toward the ship. Those on the shore joined in the cheers that sounded on the stranded

ship; but even as they cheered, a bigger wave
snatched at the boat and overturned it, dumping
all the men into the sea. The little boat was
dashed on the beach, but those who had been
rowing it bobbed about in the water until helped
to land.

A group of men, who had been talking with a
man wearing a cap trimmed with gold braid, now
carried a rope to the side of the ship and tossed
it swiftly toward land. Men on the shore were
trying to launch another boat, and every one
on the ship leaned forward watching them. The
waves carried the rope some distance forward,
and then tossed it back against the ship's side
as though playing with it, just as a cat plays with
a mouse. Tangled and twisted, the rope rose
on the crest of a high wave, then dropped from
sight, only to bob up once more, and all the time
drifting further from land.

"The vessel will be driftwood in half an hour
more! She is breaking amidships!" the man beside Jan was speaking again to the poundmaster.
"No boat can live in such a sea and no man can
swim it."

Captain Smith looked down at Jan. "It
doesn't count so much with us, Jan," he said.

"but it's the women and children. Maybe you can help them. Come!"

The dog started at the sound of command and followed his master across the water-washed deck to the group of ship's officers who were gathered around the captain of the boat. All were talking earnestly when old Captain Smith and Jan pushed between them.

"Maybe Jan can take the rope to shore," said the poundmaster, while his hand rested on Jan's wet fur. "He's a splendid swimmer and isn't afraid of the water."

The man with the gold-trimmed cap looked down at the dog whose intelligent eyes turned from face to face as though doing his best to find out why they were all looking at him, and what they wanted.

"It is too much to expect of a dog," said the man, shaking his head. "Even if he were strong enough, he could not understand."

"Jan understands everything I tell him," insisted the old man, "and it wouldn't be any harm to try him. When he once knows what we want him to do, he will do it or die in trying."

Just then the boat lurched badly and the people slipped and slid on the slanting, wet deck, but

Jan did not move. His firm muscles stiffened, he braced himself steadily and his strong back straightened. The group of officers began talking again and Jan heard them say something about his strength to Captain Smith. A heavier wave lifted the ship from the rocks then dropped her back on the jagged edges that were stabbing her to the heart, while she writhed and groaned like a living thing in agony begging for help.

The ship's captain turned his eyes on the group of women and children, then to the shore, as though he were measuring the distance across the raging water that boomed between the boat and land. Slowly he turned back to the old man and the dog.

"He may be able to do it, if you can make him understand," he said at last. Then he added in a low voice, "It is our only hope!"

Jan saw these men all were looking at him and then the ship's captain spoke.

"If the dog can reach shore with the light rope so we can attach the heavier one, we can rig up a breeches-buoy with the boatswain's chair, and the women and children could ride safely, for we could lash them to it."

Captain Smith leaned down and took Jan's

head between trembling hands. The dog and he looked into each other's eyes, and those who watched the two, felt a little thrill of hope. The animal seemed struggling to grasp the meaning of the old man's words. A bit of rope was in the captain's hand, he held it to Jan, who sniffed, then looked back at his master.

Still holding the piece of rope, Captain Smith led the dog to the side of the boat and pointed at the tangled coils that washed on the surface of the waves a short distance away.

"Go get it, Jan!" called the old man sharply.

The people on the deck crowded more closely, and the dog braced himself to spring, but just then a huge wave rose high over the vessel, the white-crested tip hissing like an angry snake, and Jan looked down, down, down into a dark hole and below it gleamed the jagged peaks of the reef, like threatening teeth of a hidden monster. He knew the danger. Drawing back he turned pleading eyes on his master.

"Go, Jan," said the voice he loved, but this time it did not command, it begged.

The big wave slipped back, others rose behind it, each one tipped with white foam, and between those waves were deep, dark hollows. **Jan** looked at them, and as he looked, something changed those white-capped things into snowy peaks of the mountains around the Hospice, while the dark places between were changed to chasms and crevasses, where Barry, Pluto, Pallas, Rex and all the dogs of the Hospice had travelled year after year for ten centuries past. He heard their voices calling him. Jan's ears cocked up, his body quivered, his muscles stiffened, his nose pointed high in the air and the cry he sent back to the calls of his kin was clear and strong like the music of a wonderful, deeptoned bell. Then he braced himself and leaped far out into the water that caught him like many strong arms and dragged him under the waves.

With all his great strength Jan fought his way to the surface and as he rose, something struck against him. He turned quickly to see what new danger threatened, and then he saw the rope and remembered what he had been told.

"Go get it, Jan!" his master had said.

The dog caught the squirming rope between his teeth, and as he did so, he heard distinctly the cheers of those on the stranded ship echoed by those on the shore before he was pulled down beneath the waves again; but he clung to the

*"Then the roaring in his ears turned to the voices of the Hospice dogs
—'The duty of a St. Bernard is to save lives!'"*

rope. When he reached the surface, Jan saw his master leaning far over the edge of the deck, pointing toward the land.

Then he understood, and without a moment's hesitation he flung his body away from the direction of the boat and faced the shore, while the rope trailed behind him, often dragging him back with terrific jerks. The force of the waves tossed him high on dizzy crests, then he was dropped swiftly into depths of seething water. His breath came in painful gasps between his tightly clinched teeth, the water rang in his ears and he was half-blinded by the stinging salt spray that cut like a sharp knife across his eyes.

In spite of his struggles he seemed no nearer the land. Back of him he could see the swaying masts of the boat, and at times the whole length of the deck with people crowded together. Jan, dazed and almost exhausted, turned to swim back to his master and safety. His paws beat the waves more feebly, but his teeth still held the rope. Down, down, down he sank, and over his head rolled the white-crested mountains of water. Then the roaring in his ears turned to the voices of the Hospice dogs. The voices of Barry

Bruno, Rex and Jan's mother sounded clearly.
Other dogs joined in the chorus until Jan knew
that he heard the voices of all the dogs that had
ever lived in the Hospice. Hundreds and hundreds of deep notes, like the bells of the Hospice
sending a message to him. "The duty of a St.
Bernard is to save lives!"

He fought with new strength, and as his head
rose above the waves, the rope still dragging
along, he heard cheers that grew nearer and
louder, but this time the voices came from the
land. A breaker curled high, dashed furiously
over him and then it carried him with a rush to
the beach and flung him, gasping and exhausted,
high on the sand, but the end of the rope was
clutched tightly between his teeth. He held it,
even when men tried to take it from him, but
the hands were kindly and as his jaws relaxed
he was lifted gently and carried where the cruel
waves could not touch him again.

Jan was too tired to open his eyes when some
one knelt beside him and stroked his wet hair,
and a man's voice said huskily, "You wonderful,
brave fellow!"

Cheers sounded loud and long, and at last
Jan opened his eyes and lifted his head wearily

for a second. Before it dropped again to the
sand, he saw men on the shore working with another, heavier rope, and some one called out,
"Thank God! They got it that time!"

Jan staggered to his feet and with wobbling
legs moved a few steps forward. Then he forgot
his weariness and aching muscles and stood
watching something strange, something that
made women near him cry, and the men cheer
wildly.

A rope reached from the shore to the stranded
ship, and something was moving slowly along
that rope toward the land. Jan's feet were in
the surf, but he did not know it as he, too,
watched and saw a chair, and in that chair was
a woman.

She was seized by eager hands and lifted down
among them, laughing and crying and saying,
"Oh, quick! Save the others!"

Again and again the chair travelled over the
waves that leaped up to clutch it, but the rope
was firm. And once when a woman was carried in the chair, a man on the shore gave a big
cry of joy as he clasped her in his arms. Jan
recognized the pretty lady, but she did not have
her baby in her arms this time. Then every one

was silent, only a woman's sob sounded softly, and the pretty lady stood staring across the water, where high above the waves swung a big leather mailbag. It came nearer and nearer, and men went far out into the surf to steady it, until it was unfastened, lifted down, opened, and the pretty lady, crying and laughing, held her baby in her arms, and the child laughed back at them all.

Men cheered and cheered, and from the ship came answering cheers, while the mother and father of the child knelt down beside the dog, saying, "You saved her, Prince Jan!"

The dog watched vainly for his master. Trip after trip brought men and women to the land, and each one was welcomed wildly. Then Jan, still watching, gave a great "Woof!" and rushed out into the water. The chair was approaching the shore, and in the chair was Jan's master. A basket was held in the old man's lap and on it was fastened a bird cage with a badly frightened canary. Through a break in the basket waved Hippity-Hop's furry paw. Those on the shore scattered as Prince Jan raced among them uttering hysterical yelps until his master stood safely beside him and leaned down catching the dog's long, soft ears and pulling them gently, while he said over and over, "Jan, Prince Jan! I knew you would do it!"

And so, ninety-one people were brought safely to shore in the boatswain's chair with the rope that Prince Jan had carried, and the baby that had ridden in the mail sack was kissed and hugged by all those who could get near her.

Then Prince Jan followed the captain, the pretty lady, and the man who walked beside her with the baby perched high on his shoulder, and who had his other arm around the waist of the baby's mother. A tiny paw reached out of the hamper Captain Smith was carrying, and the dog felt the tap of Hippity-Hop's paw on his ear. He turned at the touch and put his nose to the basket, and then he saw Cheepsie, fluttering in the cage that was gripped by the old captain's other hand.

The little party reached the top of a bluff and turned around to look across the rough waves. The deserted ship reeled sideways. Water rose and hid it an instant. When next they looked, there was nothing but the sky with threatening clouds and the wind-lashed sea.

No one spoke as they went up the pathway

of a little house where the pretty lady lived. The door was opened, they entered, and then the pretty lady knelt suddenly beside Jan and kissed his head.

"God bless you, Prince Jan!" she whispered.

And though the dog did not understand it, he was very happy because he knew they were all glad.

Chapter XIV

A Fireside Story

THAT evening, after supper, while Jan dozed in front of the fireplace with its cheerful, glowing logs, and Hippity-Hop curled in a tight ball between his paws, he did not know that the captain was telling how Jan had been brought to the pound, sick from neglect and vicious from abuse, to be killed.

The eyes of the young mother filled with tears, and she glanced from the sleeping dog to a door leading into another room, where her baby was lying, safe and warm. But when she stooped suddenly and stroked the dog's head gently, his eyes opened, his tail thumped the floor, and then Jan went to sleep again, for he was very tired.

And while he took his second nap, the father of the baby explained to the captain that he was the doctor in the little town, and had it not been for Prince Jan, the pretty little mother and her child would never have come back to the home on the bluff, after their visit to friends in California.

"Prince Jan was born in the Hospice," the old man told them. "He was only a puppy when Mr. Pixley brought him to California. To me, it never seemed just right, taking him away from the place where he belonged and where he could have been so useful, and then to treat him so cruelly. Of course, the Pixleys didn't know the truth, but that didn't help poor Jan."

The doctor turned and knelt down, studying the sleeping dog, then he rose and went back to his chair.

"I took a walking tour of Switzerland after I finished my studies in Europe," he said, at last. "So that was how I happened to be at the Hospice the day that dog was taken away. I had heard one of the monks tell about this dog's father, who died saving travellers on an ice-bridge. I went on my way toward Italy, and I saw this dog start down the trail to Martigny, the opposite direction. I have never forgotten the pitiful look in his eyes nor the call he gave as he was led away. I felt then that it was a tragedy, but never had an idea of what the poor little fellow would have to suffer. Nor had I any idea that the lives of my dear ones would be saved through him!"

"The only thing I ever knew about the St. Bernard dogs was that they lived at the Hospice and went out to hunt lost people in the snow," the captain spoke. "You are the first one I ever knew who had been there. I wish I could have seen it and those splendid dogs!"

"You know, the Pass of Great St. Bernard is the main road of travel between Italy and Switzerland," the doctor went on, and his wife leaned forward as eagerly as Jan's master to hear about Jan's birthplace. "It was through this Pass that Napoleon Bonaparte led his army of soldiers, single file and afoot, in the month of May, 1800!"

"I have read about that march," interrupted the old man, "and I know what it meant, with food and ammunition and those big guns to haul. You see, I served all through the four years of the Civil War."

"May is the most dangerous time in the Alps, for the snow melts and slides in great avalanches, often catching people with no chance for escape. When I stood on the stone steps of the Hospice, where many feet have worn little hollows, and

I remembered how many people would never have reached those steps without the dogs' help, I felt that though Napoleon was a great general and a brave man, the dogs of the Hospice were just as great and just as brave. And the monument to Barry, near the old Hospice, was as fine in my eyes as the beautiful white marble one that Napoleon built in memory of General de Sais, who died on that trip, and which is in the chapel of the Hospice. Both the general and Barry did their duty, as they saw it."

The little mother interrupted him, her eyes shining and her hands held out. "Napoleon made that march for his own glory and ambition, and to kill those who opposed his way," she said, "but Barry and the other dogs risked death each day to save lives, with no thought of gain for themselves."

"That's what I was thinking," the old captain nodded and spoke.

"What surprised me most," continued the doctor, "was that the monks who live in the Hospice do not ask pay for anything they do. The people who stop there do not even have to pay for the food that is eaten. When I asked how much I owed for shelter and food those two

days I was there, they smiled and told me there
was no charge. Of course, I could not leave in
that way, and when I insisted, I learned there
was a little box in the Monastery Chapel for
purely volunteer offerings. No one ever
watches that box, and no one is ever asked to
put anything into it. And yet," he finished
after a little pause, "often as many as five or
six hundred people have stopped at the Hospice
in one day. I was told that between twenty and
twenty-five thousand people pass over the trail
each year. Then when one remembers that for
a thousand years the ancestors of Prince Jan
have been travelling those trails and saving lives,
one can understand the splendid work of those
monks and the dogs."

"And to-day," the little mother's voice trembled, "dear old Prince Jan proved himself worthy of his ancestors and his heritage."

"Barry saved forty-two lives. His skin has
been mounted and stands, wonderfully life-like,
in the Museum of Berne," the doctor said,
thoughtfully. "He did the work in the familiar
places, the work he had been trained to do; but
to-day, there were ninety-two lives saved by
Prince Jan, with only his wonderful intelligence

to guide him through the sea and make him hold fast to that rope."

For several moments none of them spoke, but their eyes were on the dog that slept quietly at their feet, while the little three-legged kitten snuggled closely against his breast and purred loudly.

"One of the most pitiful sights at the Hospice is the House of the Dead, a short distance from the Hospice. Those who have never been identified sleep there. Sometimes, you see, the dogs and monks are too late, or the avalanches of melting snow uncover people who have been buried months, or even years. The Hospice is built on solid rock, so there is no place to dig graves. Not a tree grows within seven miles of the buildings, because it is so cold, and there is no earth for the roots. It is a bare, desolate place at all times."

"Jan must have been bewildered, going from such a place to a home in California," the little mother spoke. "And yet, see how he worked out his life and made himself worthy!"

The doctor lighted a cigar and leaned back in his big chair. "The snow at the Hospice is not like snow in other places," he finally said. "You know how, usually, it clings in masses, and when trodden upon it packs firmly; but in the Alps during a storm, the snow freezes as it falls and forms into little hard pellets. These tiny lumps of ice pile up around a traveller, and when he tries to push onward he sinks as though in a bed of quicksand. Unless help is at hand he soon is buried out of sight. The winds sweep fiercely through the passes between the mountain peaks, and send terrible, whirling clouds of snow that cut the face and blind the eyes, and many times a wanderer plunges over a precipice that he cannot see, or worn by struggles, he sinks exhausted to die. Then, there are the ice-bridges. What I am telling will give only a faint idea of the importance of the work of those magnificent dogs of the Hospice. And there is something that is not generally known, but is just as heroic. The monks who go to the Hospice volunteer for that work, knowing fully that five years up there in the altitude and intense cold mean practically the end of their lives. It ruins their lungs, and so, after a time, they go quietly down into the milder air of the Valley of the Rhone, in France, and there they wait cheerfully during the short span of life ahead of them. Only the young and strong monks are sent to the Hospice."

After the doctor ceased speaking they all sat silently and watched the blazing logs, for each of the listeners, as well as the doctor, was thinking of the sacrifice and unselfishness of those monks, and the brave loyalty of their dog-friends on the trail.

"I wish I had enough money to send Prince Jan back to his own work and home," the captain said wistfully. "Maybe, though, I can manage it some day," he added more hopefully. I feel as if he ought to be there with the others."

"You are right," agreed the doctor, and his wife nodded her head quickly. "Jan's work, his kin, his home, lie back there at the Hospice. I owe the lives of my wife and my baby to him, and if you are willing to let him go back there, I will take him back to the Hospice myself. But, won't you miss him?"

"It would make me as happy as it would make him, to know he was back there again," answered the old man eagerly, as he stooped over and caressed the dog's head.

Jan, in his sleep, recognized the touch and swished his tail lightly, but he did not open his eyes, and he never knew what the doctor and the captain had been talking about that evening.

But when it was known in the little town that the doctor was planning to take Prince Jan back to the Hospice, and those who had been saved from the ship heard the story of the dog, every one wanted to help. The newspaper printed the story of Prince Jan and his ancestors, and then people kept coming to see him, and most of them brought money for the trip back to the Hospice.

A beautiful collar of silver was made for him, and on it were engraved the words,

A Token of Gratitude from the Ninety-Two People whose Lives were Saved by Prince Jan, when All Hope Was Lost.

With this collar was a purse of money sufficient to pay Jan's passage home, and a nice sum left over to give to the monks who cared for the dogs at the Hospice.

But the biggest surprise of all came when Captain Smith found that he, too, was to make the trip to the Hospice with the doctor and Prince Jan.

The old man wrote a letter to his daughter, explaining everything and saying he would come to her as soon as he and the doctor could get back.

Jan did not know what all the excitement in the little home meant, but every one patted him or spoke kindly, and the old captain's eyes were shining all the time, as he trotted about the rooms, whistling.

Chapter XV

An Unforgotten Trail

ONCE again Jan went on a big boat, but he did not worry this time, because his friends were with him. Hippity-Hop and Cheepsie had been left with the doctor's wife until the captain should return for them.

The voyage was followed by travelling in a train, and each day of the whole journey the doctor and captain visited Jan. When he was on the train, his friends took him out of the car a number of times, so he could stretch his legs and run about on the ground while the train waited at a station. It did not take Jan long to understand that if he did not get back in the car he would be left behind. So he watched very carefully and at the first call of the captain or the doctor, he ran swiftly to the right car and jumped in it. Passengers on the long train watched him do this, for he never mistook his own car though there were several others just like the one in which he rode.

Jan wore his silver collar, and wherever he went men and women would look at it, then pat his big head and praise him. He was very happy though he did not know where he and his friends were going.

From the train they stopped at a little town, and early the next morning Jan followed the doctor and the captain to a place where a funny little cart waited them. A sleepy-looking mule was hitched to the cart, and a driver stood at the mule's head. After some talk between the driver and the doctor, the old captain climbed into the cart and the doctor trudged beside it, while the muleteer, as the drivers of these little carts are called, kept near the mule's head. At first Jan followed behind them all, but in a short time he found that the road they were trudging became more steep. Then he trotted ahead and led the way, but looked back often to see that every one was all right.

The town where they had spent the night was perched on a high bluff overlooking a noisy, scurrying little river that seemed in a great hurry to get some place else. The road Jan now travelled climbed higher and higher, but as he stopped and looked down he could see the river gurgling and hurrying along. It was a queer little stream, and the muleteer called it the Dranse. In places Jan could not see it at all, and then when he thought it had gone in another direction, it popped out, foaming and spluttering as though it thought Jan had been fooled. Sometimes it appeared to be running backward, and then suddenly it seemed to be racing forward, and always it kept playing its game of hide-and-seek with them all, and laughing and dancing like a merry elf or water-sprite. The river kept all of them interested until they stopped at a little village, which the muleteer said was Cantine de Proz.

Here they walked about, while the mule was unhitched and the little wagon was left behind. The captain now climbed on the back of the mule, and the doctor and muleteer walked on either side of him. The road had changed to a narrow, slippery pathway, one side of which dropped down to a deep chasm with a fringe of snow showing here and there.

In front of them loomed mountains, and as the path twisted sharply, Jan stopped short and stared ahead. Far away rose a huge white mountain, and around it grouped peaks of dazzling snow, the first snow Jan had seen since he was a puppy.

The doctor and the old man were watching him, but Jan did not see them. He was remembering things he had almost forgotten. Slowly the mule climbed, and the twisting trail turned and wound higher and higher. Jan lifted his head and sniffed the air that was growing colder. Then as they turned where the path seemed to end, the dog gave a loud bark and dashed ahead of them where something white lay on the ground. Faster and faster his feet flew until he stood in this white patch. His nose touched it and tossed it in little white clouds, he threw himself down and rolled over and over, then jumped to his feet and barked in sharp, excited tones. Again he snapped at it, and then he raced along the trail, frisking like a puppy, while the doctor and the captain kept smiling at each other and nodding their heads.

But not until a tiny cabin was reached, where they all went inside to rest a short time, did Prince Jan recognize the little Rest House and knew that the white trail winding up the mountain side would end at the door of the Hospice.

So, when the old man was perched again on

the mule and the travellers started toward the high white peak, Jan did not wait longer, but raced ahead of them, barking as he ran. Up, up, faster and faster, he ran. His heart pounded, his tongue hung far out of his mouth, he plunged his nose into the soft, cold drifts, sometimes stopping to take a big bite, then with yelps of joy he darted on.

And high above the steep trail rose the sharp peaks that shadowed the hundreds of deep gullies: places where the snow never melted, even in summer. And Prince Jan knew that he was following once more the path that his forefathers had trodden.

He stopped quickly and lifted his nose high, then he sent forth the great cry of the St. Bernard dogs. The deep tones echoed from crag to crag, until it sounded as if all the dogs that had ever trodden that trail were answering him.

Another twist of the pathway showed the jagged tips of the highest peaks, and just back of that crest rose the roof of the Hospice. Jan stood still for a second before he sent again that call of his people. Again he heard the voices answering, but this time the answer came from the dogs in the kennel-yards.

Jan trembled with excitement, then he shot forward and did not stop until he had reached the worn stone steps that he remembered so well. The door was closed, but some instinct made him raise his head and give the cry of the trail.

Slowly the big door swung open and Brother Antoine stood looking with puzzled eyes at a St. Bernard dog that he did not know. But Jan had not forgotten. He reared on his hind legs and let his front paws drop lightly on the shoulders of the monk. Their eyes were level, and as the dog looked at the monk, Brother Antoine called out, "Why! It is Jan—Prince Jan—come back to us!"

"Woof! Woof!" Jan's voice brought other monks hastily to the door, where Brother Antoine stood patting the big, strange dog that stood with bright shining eyes, looking from one to the other, while his fluffy tail bobbed and wagged furiously.

As they stood talking and wondering how he came there, the doctor and the captain, with the muleteer, came in sight. So the mystery was fully understood.

Inside the Hospice, the monks gathered around to listen to the story of the adventures of Prince Jan since that time when he had been led down the trail to a Land of No Snow. His silver collar was examined and admired, and Jan knew they were all glad that he had come back home.

It was Brother Antoine, though, who said, "Come with me, Prince Jan."

The big dog followed at once. Through the corridors of the Hospice, down a few steps, he went swiftly to the basement, under high archways, and through the open entrance that led into the kennel yard. And then, Jan stood once more in the home of his ancestors, and saw again his own kin.

Panting with excitement, he ran among them all and looked eagerly around. Many of the dogs were strangers to him, but when he saw old Bruno limping slowly across to where he stood, Jan's yelp made the other dogs start, and as he reached Bruno's side and showed that he had not forgotten, Bruno's joy was just as plain. Two tawny streaks flashed up to Jan, sniffed, and then yelped and yelped in wildest excitement; and this time Jan's voice mingled with his mother's and Rollo's, while the other dogs joined

until the white mountains sent back the call of the
Hospice dogs.

Brother Antoine, smiling happily, patted Jan
and left him with the other dogs. But later in
the day he returned and bade Jan follow. They
went into the Big Room where the captain and
the doctor were talking with several travellers
and two more monks. They watched the dog
move to the side of the old man; then Brother
Antoine unfastened the silver collar from Jan's
neck and hung it over the fireplace beside the
big painting of the St. Bernard dog rescuing a
man from the snow.

"It shall hang there so that all who come to
the Hospice may see it and hear the story of
Prince Jan," said Brother Antoine.

Every one praised Jan, and he then went back
to the kennel, where he was quickly surrounded
by the other dogs. It was a great day for the
St. Bernards, and they were very proud of Jan
when he told them the story of his adventures
in the strange land where there was never any
snow.

Chapter XVI

PRINCE JAN DECIDES

JAN slept soundly that night, and when he woke just before the first peep of day, and saw the other dogs stretched around him, he remembered that he was back home once more with his mother, Rollo, Bruno, and the rest of the Hospice dogs, and that now he would have a chance to do the work of his forefathers.

The soft, deep tones of the Hospice bell called them all to waken for a new day and its work. The voices of the monks singing in the chapel ceased, and at once all the dogs turned expectant eyes toward the corridor, where Brother Antoine appeared with food for their breakfast.

They leaped around the monk, or mauled each other in play, while the hot food was poured into a small trough, and soon Prince Jan was eating his share with the rest of them. They all made way for him, and there was no crowding, growling, or fighting over their morning meal.

When it was over the door leading into the yard was opened and the dogs tumbled out, barking, jumping, knocking each other over, or scampering full tilt in merry play. Rollo and his brother forgot they were grown-up and frisked together as they had done in the days before Prince Jan had been taken to the Land of No Snow.

Once more Brother Antoine stood on the steps watching them, and at last he called Jan, who trotted obediently to him, and followed through the arched corridors and the long hallway until they reached the three doors that opened, one after the other, to the outside steps.

Jan saw the doctor and the captain already there. The old man was mounted on the mule, Ketty, while Pierrot, the driver, waited beside it. The doctor held a long, stout stick.

With a bark of welcome, the dog hurried to them and stood up on his hind legs so he could lick the hand of the captain and feel its gentle touch on his head.

Brother Antoine paused at the top step and watched, but he did not speak as Pierrot called aloud and the mule started briskly down the trail leading to Martigny. The doctor walked beside the mule, and then Jan understood that they were leaving the Hospice.

He stopped and gazed back wistfully. The monk on the step gave no sign, uttered no word to call him back. Sadly Jan turned and moved along the trail behind the mule. The doctor and the captain, and even Pierrot, looked at the dog, but none of them spoke to him.

For some little distance Jan trudged heavily, then he stopped suddenly and twisted for a last look at his home. He saw the high-peaked roof and the snow-clad mountains looming above it, then he turned again to follow the travellers. They were now some distance ahead of him and a jagged cliff hid them from his eyes. Jan did not move.

Through a gap he saw the captain, the doctor, and the guide. They halted this time. They were waiting there for him.

The dog started quickly toward them, but something made him look again where Brother Antoine stood on the steps. Jan hesitated, then he sat down facing the trail toward Martigny. In a few minutes he saw the little procession start on its way. He knew he could catch up with them easily if he ran fast, but still he sat without moving, his eyes fastened on that gap between the mountains.

He lifted his head and sent out the cry of his forefathers, so that the echoes rang again and again. The answering voices died away, there was no sound save the swish of melting snow that slipped down the steep places, and then Prince Jan, St. Bernard, turned and trotted up the trail to the home of his ancestors.

Brother Antoine waited on the top step. As the dog reached him, the monk stooped and patted him, whispering softly, "It is not easy, Prince Jan, when the paths that Love and Duty travel lie far apart."

And so Prince Jan came back to the work of his ancestors, and as the months passed by he saved many lives and was very happy. The young dogs listened in respectful wonder when he told of the strange places and things that he had found in the Land of No Snow. They learned from him the lessons of obedience, loyalty, and kindliness.

"If you do the very best you know how, it will always work out right in the end," Jan ended each talk.

But sometimes at night as he slept among the

other dogs, he saw the captain walking about a room. Cheepsie was perched on the old man's shoulder, while Hippity-Hop skipped beside them, and the dog knew that they were thinking of him.

Then Jan's ears cocked up, his tail swished gently on the stone floor of the Hospice, for in his dreams he heard the faint sound of a quavering voice singing:

"Old dog Tray is ever faithful,
Grief cannot drive him away.
He's gentle and he's kind
And you'll never, never find
A better friend than old dog Tray."

Chapter XVII

JAN'S REWARD

TWO years went past and Jan's work at the Hospice brought him great happiness, for he knew that he was doing the work of his ancestors and living a useful life.

Often as he travelled the snow trails, he remembered the Land of No Snow, the warm sunshine, the fragrant flowers and the beautiful trees laden with golden fruit. But the one thing for which his loyal heart yearned most was the touch of a wrinkled hand on his head and the sound of the old poundmaster's voice. No one knew Jan's thoughts, for he was always eager to do his work the best he knew how, and to teach the puppies to be proud of the privilege of helping people.

Brother Antoine had left the Hospice and gone down into the warmer climate of the Valley of the Rhone. His work had been done bravely and unselfishly, and the monks had asked that he be sent to a place where sunshine and milder air would give him a chance to recover his strength and prolong his life. Jan greatly missed this dear friend.

There were cold mornings when Prince Jan rose stiffly, for he had not been hardened to the trail work from puppy days as Rollo and the other dogs had been. Five years of warm sunshine in the Land of No Snow had made Jan's muscles soft and flabby and he felt the cold weather more than any of the other St. Bernards. Then, too, his long hair made the work of the trails harder for him because the snow clung to his fur and when it melted and soaked to his skin, the monks watched carefully to keep him from becoming chilled. Once or twice he had limped badly after coming in from his work, and then he had been rubbed and taken into the Big Room and allowed to stretch before the fireplace, and for a while he was not sent out with the other dogs.

One day during summer many of the dogs were given a chance to exercise outdoors. Jan sat watching the youngsters tumble each other about, while he recalled the times when he and Rollo had played that way and old Bruno had sat watching them. Then one of the pups began barking, and soon the others added their calls of welcome as a little party of travellers appeared in the opening of the mountain pass toward Martigny. Jan, mindful of his responsibility, joined in the calls. His deep, mellow tones sounded distinctly above the others, but he did not know that those on the trail had stopped while an old man, mounted on a mule, cried out, "Listen! That is Jan! I know his voice!"

A younger man and a young woman who were also mounted on mules, laughed happily, though the woman's eyes were filled with tears as she looked at the old man. Then they hurried on and soon were in plain sight of the steps that led into the Hospice. In a few more minutes the mules stopped and the dogs crowded about to show how glad they were to have visitors.

The old man climbed down from his mule and turned to face the dogs. He looked quickly from one to the other, until he found the one he sought. Prince Jan started, his eyes lighted up suddenly, his head was lifted high, then with a yelp of joy the big dog leaped forward.

"Jan! Jan! You haven't forgotten me, have

you?" cried the old poundmaster, kneeling down and putting his arms about the shaggy neck, while the dog's rough tongue licked the wrinkled hand, and little whimpers of delight told of Jan's happiness.

The other dogs crowded around in excitement, wondering what it all meant, and the guide, with the lady and gentleman, now beside the old man, kept talking together and patting Jan's head. But he did not think of them as they moved to the door, for Jan's only thought was to keep closely beside his dear old master whose hand rested on the furry head, and whose kindly, faded blue eyes were filled with tears of joy. Jan's eyes spoke his own happiness and love.

In the Big Room the monks received the old captain, whom they had not forgotten, and after the first greetings were over, they listened to the story of the poundmaster's homesickness for Jan. The lady, who was the captain's daughter, explained that the mines in far-away Alaska had been sold for enough money to build a home in Southern California, where the captain lived with them. But it had not taken her very long to learn how much her father wished to see Prince Jan once more. So the little family had travelled back to Jan's home in the Alps.

That evening Jan was very happy as he stretched before the fireplace at the captain's feet. He did not sleep, for his eyes were fixed on the old man's face, and when the poundmaster reached down to touch Jan's head, the dog's tail swished and thumped. Then Jan rose to his feet and laid his head on the captain's knee, just as he used to do in the other days.

The monks talked very earnestly with the captain's daughter and her husband, and at last they all sat down together, smiling at Jan. He did not understand what they were saying but he knew they were very happy, and he was happy with them.

What they had talked about was their plan for the dog. He was now past eight years old and in a short time would not be able to go out on the trail. Prince Jan had done his part in the work of the St. Bernards with honor to himself and to them, and now that he was growing old, the monks felt that he was entitled to spend his last years in comfort and happiness with his old friend, Captain Smith.

So, the next morning Jan was brought to the

entrance of the Hospice, and there, as before, he saw Captain Smith on the mule. The captain's daughter and her husband were mounted on the other mules, and the guide had started along the trail.

Jan looked at the monks who were grouped on the stone steps, then he looked at the captain. The mules moved slowly behind the guide. Prince Jan gave a pitiful little whimper as he saw them go. Then he heard the voice of the monk who now had charge of the kennels.

"Go on, Jan!"

The dog took a few steps and stopped. The monks were smiling and pointing toward the trail that led to Martigny. He turned and watched those who were riding down that trail. They reached the gap and paused.

Jan stood with trembling body, his eyes filled with longing and grief. Then clear and strong he heard the voice he loved.

"Come on, Jan! We're going home now!"

"Woof! Woof!" the answer woke the echoes sleeping in the hearts of the mountains, the dogs of the Hospice took up the call of their kin, and the big dog dashed swiftly along the trail until he reached the little group.

Leaping up, he licked the poundmaster's hand. Then with head erect, Prince Jan, for the last time, travelled the trail of his ancestors. He did not know where he was going, but it made no difference to him. His master was looking down at him and smiling.

THE END